D

Mathangi Subramanian is a writer, educator, and activist who believes that stories have the power to change the world. A former American public school teacher, assistant vice president at Sesame Workshop and senior policy analyst at the New York City Council, she has received numerous awards, including a Fulbright-Nehru Fellowship, a Teachers College Office of Policy and Research Fellowship and a Jacob Javits Fellowship. Her nonfiction has appeared in publications such as *The Hindu Sunday Magazine, Quartz, Al Jazeera America, Feministing* and the Seal Press anthology *Click!: When We Knew We Were Feminists*. Her fiction has appeared in *Kahani, Skipping Stones* and *The Hindu's Young World*. *Dear Mrs. Naidu* is her first novel.

Dear Mrs. Naidu

MATHANGI SUBRAMANIAN

For Ellen
MSdr
12/2016

young
zubaan

YOUNG ZUBAAN
an imprint of Zubaan Publishers Pvt Ltd
128 B Shahpur Jat, 1st floor
NEW DELHI 110 049
Email: contact@zubaanbooks.com
Website: www.zubaanbooks.com

First published by Zubaan 2015

10 9 8 7 6 5 4 3 2 1
ISBN 978 93 83074 98 3

Zubaan is an independent feminist publishing house based in New Delhi with a strong academic and general list. It was set up as an imprint of India's first feminist publishing house, Kali for Women, and carries forward Kali's tradition of publishing world quality books to high editorial and production standards. *Zubaan* means tongue, voice, language, speech in Hindustani. Zubaan is a non-profit publisher, working in the areas of the humanities, social sciences, as well as in fiction, general non-fiction, and books for children and young adults under its Young Zubaan imprint.

Typeset by Jojy Phillip, New Delhi 110 015
Printed at Raj Press, R-3 Inderpuri, New Delhi 110 012.

For
A. Kumaraswamy and P.K. Swarnambal
(Better known as Thatha Patti)

"Do not think of yourselves as small girls. You are the powerful Durgas in disguise.... Forget about the earth. You shall move the skies."

– Sarojini Naidu, 1930

June 10, 2013

Dear Mrs. Naidu,

I guess you're wondering why I'm writing you this letter.

Honestly, Mrs. Naidu, so am I.

Amma says I'm not allowed to speak to strangers. You would think that also meant that I shouldn't write to them. But since this is a school assignment, she says it's okay.

(Here is a tip, Mrs. Naidu: if you ever want adults to let you do something, just tell them it is a school assignment. They will one hundred percent agree to it every time.)

Maybe I should start from the beginning.

The beginning was last week.

Last week I started Class Six and I met our new teacher, Annie Miss, who is not like any teacher I have had before.

For example: Annie Miss says she doesn't think school should be about memorizing things and saying them back. She says memorizing things and saying them back makes you a parrot, not a person. She says she wants us to grow our brains *and* our hearts.

When she said that, I wanted to ask how growing our hearts will help us pass our exams and get into college and get a job and buy a house with a proper roof and maybe even a garden, which are all the reasons why I go to school. But I didn't.

You know how adults are, Mrs. Naidu. They don't like questions.

Even though it was only the first week of school, Miss gave us an assignment. (Miss says that now we are in sixth standard, it is time for us to be serious. Every teacher says this every year. But none of them ever gave us assignments during the first week of school, so Annie Miss might mean it.)

The assignment is to write letters to someone we would like to get to know better. She said that we could pick anyone, as long as we explain why.

As you have probably concluded, Mrs. Naidu, I picked you.

(This is the first time I have ~~said~~ written the word "concluded." It's an English word that means "figured out based on clues and evidence." I learned it by reading detective stories, even though our English Miss says they are useless rags. ~~I think this proves~~ I conclude that she is wrong.)

I understand if you find this confusing, Mrs. Naidu. After all, you and I don't have much in common. For one thing, I am alive and you are – well, you are not.

(I'm sorry if that was rude, but I've never written to a ~~dead~~ ~~deceased~~ ~~passed on~~ historical person before, so I don't really know the polite way to say ~~that you are dead~~ it.)

Here's another difference between us. When you were twelve – which is how old I am now – you wrote a poem that was thousands of lines long. And it was in English.

I don't think I could write that many lines in *any* language. Definitely not in English.

Also, when you were twelve, you topped the Madras University matriculation exam.

I topped our Class Five exams, but I don't think I could top a college exam, even if I studied really, really hard.

You fought for India's freedom and won.

I've never fought for anything. If I did, I'm not sure if I would win. Especially if I was fighting against the Britishers, who have lots of spies and detectives and things that I don't think we have in India.

You lived in a huge house with a lot of rooms and maids to do your housework.

My house has only one room, and Amma *is* a maid who does other people's housework.

You had a lot of brothers and sisters and then you had a lot of kids.

I don't have *any* brothers and sisters. (I don't have

kids either, but you probably ~~know~~ concluded that already, since I'm only twelve.)

Here is why I decided to write to you: I'm reading a book about your life. Vimala Madam gave it to me – or, she gave it to Amma to give to me.

I haven't read all of it yet – it's in English, but much more complicated English than the kind they use in detective stories, so it's taking me some time. So far, I've only read the part about your childhood. But that part makes me like you.

When you were my age, or even younger, Mrs. Naidu, it seems like you stood up to parents and teachers and all the adults who don't understand anything at all, but act like they do. For example, the book says that your parents wanted you to speak English instead of Bengali. It says you locked yourself in a room for a whole day because you disagreed with them. You didn't even come down for lunch.

I don't know if this is true or just a story, but if I had a house with more than one room, there are plenty of times I would've locked myself behind a closed door.

I guess that's why you seem like someone who understands kids like me. Like maybe you wouldn't mind if I asked you questions and read detective stories and stayed at school late so I didn't have to go to Vimala Madam's house.

And now I have completed my first assignment,

which is to introduce myself to the person that I am writing to.

To be completely honest, my brain and my heart feel exactly the same as when I started.

All the best,
Sarojini

P.S. This reminds me of something we *do* have in common – we have the same first name.

June 14, 2013

Dear Mrs. Naidu,

Our next assignment is to write about someone who is important to our lives.

For me, that's easy. The most important person in my life is Amma.

Mrs. Naidu, I may not have much in common with you, but Amma definitely does. Amma is a fighter, and she loves words. She hasn't written poems that have been published in books, like yours, and she hasn't fought for anything as serious as getting the Britishers out of India. But when someone needs help or is not being treated fairly, Amma always steps in, and she always finds the right words.

Like, for example, Amma found the right words to get a water truck to come every day when the tap in our area stopped working. She found the right words to get the bank to let Amma and Tasmiah Aunty open bank accounts without their husbands having to sign for them. She found the right words to get the school to enroll Roshan even though his Amma, Hema Aunty, didn't have his birth certificate. And then she found the right words to get Roshan a birth certificate so he wouldn't have that problem ever again.

Sometimes Amma makes things right without even using words. Like when we're on the bus and a man says something he shouldn't be saying or touches something he shouldn't be touching, Amma gives him this look. It's like she has laser beams coming out of her eyes.

(I read about laser beams in a comic book about an evil genius who wants to take over the world. Laser beams are like long pieces of light that are sharp on the edges. I know that ~~when you were alive during your time~~ you've probably never seen them, so you might not be able to picture what I'm talking about. But trust me, you don't want to get caught at the end of a laser beam. Especially when that laser beam comes from Amma's eyes.)

When Amma looks at you, it doesn't matter how strong or important or confident you are. You stop doing what you're doing. Sometimes you even apologize.

Amma knows what to say during a fight. But she also knows what to say after one. Like once, Amir and I were playing outside, and some boys came up to us and started calling Amir names and telling him he shouldn't play with me. They said that Muslim boys like Amir who like to play with Hindu girls like me should leave India.

(Actually, they didn't say 'leave India.' They said something much worse.)

(But I don't want to write that here, Mrs. Naidu. Partly because I don't want to offend you, and partly because I don't want to remember.)

Amir and I came inside, and we were both crying. Amma was squeezing tamarind for sambar. When she hugged us, the palms of her hands were sticky and damp.

She said to Amir, "Sarojini and I will always love you. Wherever we are, that's where you belong."

Amir wiped his face and even smiled. I don't know how Amma knew that was the right thing to say, but it was. Amir and I felt cozy and safe the rest of the night, even though those boys were outside doing all kinds of things that you would not approve of, Mrs. Naidu.

So like I was saying, Amma always finds the right words.

Well, not always.

There was one time when she didn't find the right words. And it changed both of our lives forever, even though my life hadn't even started yet.

Amma grew up on a farm. When she talks about it, it sounds magical and perfect, like one of your poems.

(Mrs. Naidu, I don't completely understand all your poems. But I like the way they sound when I say them out loud. Do you think that it's okay to like things that you don't understand?)

I wish I could visit the farm. Amma says that at night, it would be hard to sleep because the frogs and the crickets kept croaking and chirping. She says after it rained, the sky would be so blue and the earth so green that it hurt your eyes. She says that after school, she and her sisters used to climb the gooseberry trees and shake the branches until all the fruit came down, or until they got caught by their older cousins who said climbing trees was unladylike.

I wish we could go visit. I wish I could hear the frogs and the crickets and feel the tree branches scratch the bottoms of my feet and maybe even taste some gooseberries.

But Amma can't go back. And she can't take me.

Because Amma married Appa.

That's another thing you and Amma have in common, Mrs. Naidu: you both had love marriages. You both met your husbands when you were teenagers. You both wanted to marry men who were from different castes.

Your story is different from Amma's though. I read that when you were fifteen, your Appa sent you to England to study, to keep you from getting married.

(No offense, Mrs. Naidu, but if I thought Amma

would send me to the UK to keep me away from a boy, I would pretend to be in love with Amir just so I could go.)

Eventually, though, your Appa said it was fine. I guess he had to, because he helped pass the law that made it okay to marry someone from another caste, and if he was letting everyone else in India do it he had to let you do it too. But then I think that he also probably said yes because he loved you and wanted you to be happy.

(I'm actually still at the part where you're studying in England, but I skipped ahead a little bit just to see what happened.)

It seems to me, Mrs. Naidu, that you fought for your marriage and you won. You found the right words, and then you and your husband lived happily ever after.

Amma fought for her marriage too. But she didn't find the right words. She didn't win. And she and Appa didn't live happily ever after.

Amma married Appa. Then Amma's sisters and her Amma and her Appa and her cousins and her uncles and her aunts and everybody she knew stopped talking to her. So she and Appa decided to leave the village, because even the frogs and the crickets weren't loud enough to drown out the silence.

So Amma and Appa moved to Bangalore. Then,

when I was two years old, Appa left. I'm pretty sure he's still alive, because Amma still wears her thali. Sometimes I think he might have started another family, probably with a lot of sons.

Amma never talks about him. And I don't ask.

Well, I did ask, once. Sort of. I asked Amma if she wishes she had stayed on the farm, with the gooseberries and the frogs and the sisters. She told me, "If I had stayed, I wouldn't have you."

If you notice, Mrs. Naidu, this didn't actually answer the question.

All the best,
Sarojini

June 18, 2013

Dear Mrs. Naidu,

My next assignment is to talk about where I am from. I guess I should tell you about my neighbourhood.

Mrs. Naidu, I know you grew up in Hyderabad, which is the biggest city in Andhra Pradesh, and also the capital. I live in Bangalore, also known as Bengaluru, which is the biggest city in Karnataka, and also the capital. I know that you ~~loved~~ love your city even though it might be noisy and crowded and polluted and sometimes a little bit backwards. That makes me think that you understand that even though a place can have a lot of problems, it can still be home.

Just like you love your home, I love mine.

This may sound funny because most people see my home and hold their noses or shake their heads or get really angry for a second.

Well, not most people. *Most* people don't notice my home, even when they stand right in front of it.

My home is in a coconut grove that's squished between a brand new hospital and a shopping mall full of western stores. Amma says that if it wasn't for all the trees, someone would have come and bulldozed it a long time ago and built another shopping mall. When I said that it doesn't make sense to build a new shopping mall next to an old one, she said that in Bangalore, you can never have too many shopping malls.

(I know, Mrs. Naidu. I don't understand either.)

Most of the time, I love my home and I love my neighbourhood. But the rest of the time, I wish I could run away to a house like yours, a house so comfortable and humongous and posh that you called it the Golden Threshold, which is also the name of your first book of poems.

Here are the reasons why I sometimes don't love my neighbourhood. For one thing, most of us don't have proper roofs. We cover our houses with pieces of blue plastic, or sheets of tin, or whatever else we can find. Hema Aunty's roof, for example, is a hoarding with a photo of a woman politician with a round, fair face. Hema Aunty says that the politician promised everyone new roofs when she ran for election, so it was only fair to take the hoarding and help her keep her promise. Anyway, when it rains (and it rains a *lot*) all of our stuff gets soggy and the paths between our houses become one big muddy puddle and the trash that people throw outside starts stinking even more than it usually does.

But then, even though everything's always wet, there's never any water to drink. I mean, we have a tap, but it only works half the time, and in the summer, when we're the thirstiest, it hardly works at all. That means we have to walk to the truck and fill up drums and drag them all the way home when we're supposed to be getting ready for work or school. If the truck comes late and we miss it, we're dirty and thirsty all day.

Also, there are a lot of dogs in the neighbourhood, which some people don't like.

(I know you wouldn't think that, Mrs. Naidu – you had so many pet dogs and cats that I can't keep track of all their names. And I'm still at the beginning of your life!)

I guess people think that the dogs in my area are scary. Although, to be fair, they also think the people in my area are scary. They even think us kids are scary, because we might get them sick or something.

If I become rich, I'll probably move away, just like Amir did, and just like everyone does the second they make enough money.

But sometimes I think I'd rather stay here and fix all the problems. I'd put cement down so we had real roads. I'd put pipes in so we could have water all the time. I'd get us a generator that we could all share, so we could stay warm in the rain. I'd ask the garbage collectors to come take the trash and I'd make sure every house had a roof.

(I'd probably keep the dogs, though. They're not so bad. Maybe I would even teach them to fight crime, just like bloodhounds in detective stories.)

Like I said, Mrs. Naidu, most of the time, I love where I live. Like when we run out of cooking gas, and Mary Aunty lends us some to get us through the month. Or when Amina Aunty's house floods, and Amma makes hot bhaji and invites her and her children over to warm up. Or when Hema Aunty's husband disappears and everyone knows he's going to come back home with blurry eyes and hot, nasty breath, and Kamala Aunty starts singing bhajans in her sweet, clear, mynah-bird voice to help us all think about something else.

Or when there's enough water, and all the families do laundry at once and hang it up between the houses. Then our neighbourhood looks like a tropical bird flew by and dropped all its feathers. It even smells good, like soap and cloth and sunlight and something else clean and fresh and hopeful.

And even though I wish we didn't have to get water from the big yellow truck, sometimes that can be fun too.

Especially when your best friend helps you and you have contests to see who can take the most and who can do it fastest.

And when your Amma and your best friend's Amma watch you scrambling past each other and laugh so hard they have to bend over and hold their stomachs.

And when you win, and your best friend's older brothers slap him on the back and ask him what it feels like to be beaten by a girl.

And when your best friend smiles and says, "She's not a girl. She's Sarojini."

And when you all go inside and drink Tasmiah Aunty's hot hot chai in three quick gulps so that you have time to change into your uniform before you walk to school and spend the whole day together.

How could you not like a home like that?

All the best,
Sarojini

June 22, 2013

Dear Mrs. Naidu,

I have some good news. Miss just gave me marks back for these letters. She says that I am doing a good job and that I am writing 'from the heart.'

I guess that means that my heart is growing.

(No offense to Miss, but I really hope my brain is growing too.)

I'm not telling you about my marks to brag, Mrs. Naidu. I'm telling you because I want to thank you for helping with my assignment. I think 'writing from the heart' means something like writing honestly. It's easy to write honestly when I'm writing to a ~~listener~~ reader friend like you.

Today, we have to write about something that happened this summer. If you remember, Mrs. Naidu, I mentioned that I have a best friend named Amir. He used to live next door to us. Well, not next door exactly – there was a wall between us, but we shared the same roof. A roof which used to be a blue sheet, but now is made out of tin.

Amir and I do everything together. I think it's because we fill in the parts of each other that are missing. I help him with maths and English and he helps me with social studies and science. He taught me how to bowl and I taught him how to bat. When his brothers shout and fight, he comes over to our house and we sing songs and tell stories. When Amma's salary doesn't quite last the whole month, he brings over roti-subzi.

I never tell him when we're hungry, and he never tells me when he's scared.

That's the best thing about me and Amir. We both just know.

Some people think it's strange that we have so much in common, because if you look at us from the outside, Amir and I seem like opposites.

I'm a girl and he's a boy.

I'm a Hindu and he's a Muslim.

I'm an only child and he has two brothers.

All those opposites don't matter, though, because inside we're the same.

(Maybe it has something to do with the way our hearts grew in the same place at the same time. Miss might know.)

Mrs. Naidu, I'm very sorry, but I just realized I made a mistake in this letter. I am writing in the present tense. I should be writing in the past tense.

(I learned about past tense in class. Which is probably why I forgot it. Things you learn in school hardly ever make sense in real life.)

What I wrote about is how Amir and I were before.

But it's not before any more. Now, it's after.

Things started changing from before to after when Amir's brother Farooq got a job at a call centre. They changed even more when Amir's brother Tariq finished his engineering degree and started working at this manufacturing company with a foreign name.

At first the changes were small and they were nice. Like getting a tin roof. Or being able to buy chocolates on the way home from school on Fridays before Amir went to mosque.

Then, this summer, the changes were bigger. Amir and his family moved into a flat in a neighbourhood that had paved roads that didn't wash away every time it rained. Their house had water that came straight out of the taps and a bedroom with a door.

Even the big changes were nice at first. We would go to Amir's house when it was really hot and we would lie on the floor under the ceiling fan, which worked most of the time. Farooq bought a two-wheeler, and on Sundays he took us to Gangarams and let us buy one book each, and then he took us to Lal Bagh where we all sat under the trees and read and ate kulfi from the vendors that walk around the lake.

Then the biggest change happened and it wasn't nice at all.

Amir switched schools.

He started going to a private school. And not just any private school: Greenhill Public School. It's the same school that Vimala Madam's kids went to, and Vimala Madam is rich.

Just like you.

Just like Amir.

But not like me.

As you know, rich and poor are opposites, Mrs. Naidu.

I guess they might the biggest opposites of all.

You probably think I'm silly for being surprised. I just thought that Amir and I would always be friends. And I guess we are still friends. But it's not the same.

For one thing, Amir hardly comes to ~~our~~ my neighbourhood any more. Both of our Ammas say it's safer in Amir's neighbourhood. Amir and I don't play cricket outside like we used to, because we don't know any of the kids on ~~the~~ Amir's street. Once when I knocked on the door, Tasmiah Aunty said Amir wasn't home because he was buying school supplies, even though every year that I can remember, we've always bought our school supplies together.

We don't do our homework together any more either – Amir's is really different than mine. And it's all in English. Plus, Amir has all these new friends now. I see him with them sometimes when I'm walking home from school. He always waves at me, and I always wave back, but we never walk towards each other like we used to.

When Amir and I went to the same school, we used to wear out our school uniforms until they fell apart. Have you ever seen worn out uniforms, Mrs. Naidu? The fabric gets so thin that if you hold it up to the light, you can almost see through it. That's how Amir and I feel now: stretched and worn out and scratchy.

So that's what happened this summer. I didn't exactly lose my best friend. But I didn't exactly keep him either.

All the best,
Sarojini

June 26, 2013

Dear Mrs. Naidu,

Mrs. Naidu, I just realized that in my last letter, I was very selfish. I was talking about myself the whole time, and I didn't even ask you: did you ever have a best friend?

(I know this is breaking my policy of not asking questions to adults. But I think since you are ~~dead passed away no longer alive~~ historical, maybe, technically, you are not like other adults. I hope you don't mind.)

I know you had lots of friends, Mrs. Naidu. Like Gandhi Thatha and Panditji and lots of other people who I will probably learn about in social studies. You even wrote letters to them, which people don't really do anymore since they can text or talk on the phone instead.

But did you ever have a *best* friend, Mrs. Naidu?

A friend that made all your other friends less important?

A friend that was so close to you that he could just look at you and know exactly what you were feeling?

A friend that you had so much fun with that you didn't need any other friends?

If you remember from my last letter, Mrs. Naidu, I ~~have had~~ maybe have a best friend that makes all my other friends less important.

So when Miss told us that our next assignment was to write about a time we made a new friend, at first I couldn't think of anyone.

But then, this morning, that changed.

I was walking to school, and I was kind of hurrying, because I was late from going to the water truck and then I realized that I had forgotten my pencil case and so I had to go back and get it... anyway, you get the idea.

So I was walking to school, and I was kind of hurrying, when suddenly I heard, "Oy!"

Mrs. Naidu, where I live, everyone knows each other. We may never speak to each other or even look at each other, but we know each other. Do you what that means?

It means that everyone knows that I am Sarojini and my Appa doesn't live with us and my Amma had a love marriage and works in rich people's houses and I go to the government school and Amma and I ~~share~~ used to share a wall with a Muslim family and that we just got a tin roof last year.

I guess it's only fair, because I know the same things about them.

Who their parents are. What their problems are. What everyone says about them.

So when someone yells "Oy!" I don't turn around, because you don't yell "Oy!" to someone you know.

But then, it happened again.

"Oy!"

This time I looked. Not to see who was making the noise, but to see who wasn't answering.

I found the person making the noise first. It was a girl in a purple and gold pavade – or, what used to be purple and gold, I guess, but now looks kind of gray. Her hair was oily and dusty, and her skin was the colour of the ground when it's soaked with fresh rain. She had a little boy on her hip. When she yelled "Oy!" for the third time, I realized that she was looking right at me.

"Are you oy-ing me?" I asked.

"Do you see anyone else here?" she said, rolling her eyes. (Which, if you'll notice Mrs. Naidu, is not an answer but another question.)

"Um," I said. "No, I um – I guess not."

"Where do you go to school?" she asked.

I looked down at my uniform, which is the same uniform that all the government school kids wear, and then I looked back at her.

"Well?" She hitched the boy up a little farther onto her hip.

"Ambedkar Government School," I said.

"Do they have an anganwadi?" she asked.

"Ang-an-what-i?" I said.

"A place for kids like him," she said.

"I don't know," I said. "I'm in sixth class."

"Me too," she said, which was another surprise, because she's probably half my height and she's skinny enough to fit between the pages of a comic book. I guess she knew what I was thinking, because then she said, "At least, I should be."

"You're not in school?" I said.

"That's what I just said," she told me, rolling her huge, tired eyes. Even though she was speaking Kannada, she sounded funny. There was something about the way the sounds all mushed together like bisebele bath in her mouth, and how she didn't keep using English words in between the Kannada ones.

That's when I remembered where I had seen her.

"You're one of those country kids that live at the construction site," I said. "The one behind the hospital."

"Me and all the other kids who don't go to school," she said.

"What do you mean?" I asked.

"Well, I don't know about the others. But me, if I go to school, no one's going to watch him," she said, sticking out her chin like she was pointing to the boy. "So I have to stay back."

"Can't you leave him with your parents?" I asked. I had seen a lot of children playing in the piles of sand next to construction sites, or toddling around the cement floors while their mothers and fathers carried bags of heavy rocks on their heads.

"Do you know how many kids get killed in accidents at these places?" she said, shivering. "As much as he drives me mad, I don't want him to die."

And she turned and – really, Mrs. Naidu, I'm not making this up – she spat! I've never seen a twelve-year-old girl do that before, at least not in that way – the way that men do, without apologizing or looking embarrassed or anything.

When she did that, Mrs. Naidu, a voice in my head told me to stop talking to her and walk away. I couldn't blame the voice (which, by the way, sounded suspiciously like Amma, or maybe Hema Aunty.) After all, let's review the clues so far:

1. She lives at a construction site.
2. She is from a village.
3. She doesn't go to school.
4. She spits like a man.

I know a detective would conclude that this girl is poor, backwards, lazy and impolite, and that an Aunty would conclude that well-behaved girls like me shouldn't be speaking to her.

Maybe you feel the same way, Mrs. Naidu. But there was something about her that I liked. I'm not sure what it was, exactly – maybe the fact that she seemed like a fighter, like you or Amma.

Besides, every good detective knows that sometimes you have to ignore the clues and follow your instincts.

So that's what I did.

I said, "I'm going to school right now. Do you want to come?"

She shrugged like she didn't care, but I could tell that she did. Then she started walking beside me, the boy still on her hip.

After a few blocks, we got to the school, and I stopped in front of the gate.

"Is this it?" she asked.

"Yes," I said.

"Oh," she said.

I knew what she meant.

We have some nice teachers at our school, Mrs. Naidu, but we don't have a nice building. For one thing, there is a weirdly-shaped hole in the gate. (A bunch of boys tried to break the padlock by running their scooter into it. I think they're probably the ones who were mean to Amir, but I'm not sure.) For another thing, it smells funny, probably because the walls are lined with garbage where people drop their plastic wrappers and empty beer cans and old newspapers. The school compound is full of small, sharp rocks that sneak through the holes in your shoes and sting and slice your feet. In the summer, it gets really dusty, and when we eat outside or play shuttlecock, we can't stop sneezing. The compound is slightly sloped, so during monsoon, dirt rolls down the hill and floods our classrooms with muddy, brown sludge.

"Come on," I said, "I'll introduce you to Annie Miss."

"Who?" she asked.

"My teacher," I said. Then I looked at her sideways and said, "You ask a lot of questions."

She shrugged, hitched the boy up, and said, "Let's go."

As usual, when we got to the classroom, Annie Miss was already there.

Well, it's usual for Annie Miss, but it's not usual for our school. A lot of teachers show up late, or they don't show up at all. But Miss is always early, drawing on the board and putting out papers and sometimes even sweeping when the ayah doesn't come. She stays late too. I think maybe she sleeps there, but I can't be sure.

Plus her classroom looks different. It's only the beginning of the year, but she already has a lot of the work we've done up on the walls. She's got a bookshelf with a whole bunch of books that she brings from home. This morning, she was reading one that had a bright red cover and had some English words on it that I don't understand, like "social justice" and "pedagogy." Once Roshan asked her what the books were about, and she said, "Creating a more just and beautiful world." I don't know what that means, Mrs. Naidu, but I've never seen any of our other teachers reading books in English – or any other language for that matter.

"Good morning, Sarojini," Miss said, putting a piece of paper in her book and closing it.

"Good morning, Miss," I said. "This is… um…"

"Deepti," the girl said, switching the boy to her other hip. "And this is my brother, Abhi. We want to go to school here."

"Is that right?" Miss said.

"But we don't have any papers," Deepti said. "Or money."

"This is a government school," Miss said. "All you need to come here is a brain and a heart. Do you have those?"

"Yes, Miss," Deepti said, straightening up. "Yes, I do. I mean, we both do."

"Then you are welcome here," Miss said. "How old are you?"

"Twelve," Deepti said.

"How long since you've been in school?"

"About three months."

"Where did you go to school before that?"

"First Gulbarga," Deepti said. (That explained the accent.) "Then Bangalore."

"Where in Bangalore?"

Deepti shuffled her feet a little bit and said, "Peenya, Hebbal, Marathahalli…" Her voice trailed off, but I don't think she was finished.

"That's a lot of schools," Miss said.

"I'm smart, Miss," Deepti said. "In Gulbarga I was first rank. I can be first rank here too, if I just stay in one place."

"Sarojini," Miss said, turning to me. "If Deepti joins us, would you help her learn what she's missed?"

"Yes, Miss," I said.

"Deepti, will you work with Sarojini?"

Deepti shrugged, and I think she was a little embarrassed, but she said, "Alright."

"Good. Now, how old is your brother?"

"Four."

"Come with me," Miss said. "Sarojini, as students come in, please tell them to compare answers on last night's assignment."

"Yes, Miss," I said.

As they were leaving, Deepti turned around and said, "Oy, Sarojini!"

I looked up, startled.

"Thanks," she said. And then she smiled.

And I couldn't help it. I smiled right back.

You know what, Mrs. Naidu? I think my heart grew a little bit right then.

All the best,
Sarojini

July 1, 2013

Dear Mrs. Naidu,

Today Miss wants us to write about a time when we tried something new. She says that trying new things is good for both our hearts *and* our brains because it makes us feel and think in ways we never felt or thought before.

So it's very lucky that I tried something new yesterday.

It's lucky for my heart and for my brain, and it's especially lucky for this assignment.

It started because of a new rule Amma made. You might remember, Mrs. Naidu, that I used to live next door to my best friend.

If you were paying attention, you know that ~~two things are~~ one thing about that statement is definitely different and another thing is maybe different now.

The thing that is definitely different is that my best friend doesn't live next door to me anymore. Now he lives next door to someone else, who probably also has running water and ceiling fans and a brother with a two-wheeler.

The thing that is maybe different is that maybe I don't have a best friend any more.

Anyway, I was talking about the new rule. The new rule is that after school, I cannot go home, because the house is empty and somebody might take advantage of me.

(I still don't know what 'take advantage' means, but it's something bad. I mostly hear it from the aunties in our neighbourhood who yell at their daughters a lot.)

So now, instead of going home, I have to meet Amma at the last house she works in every day.

Mrs. Naidu, if Amma worked in your house, I wouldn't mind. I bet you would invite me in and make me tea and read me poems. You might even tell me stories about what it's like to be in a British jail or to sail around the world.

But unfortunately, Mrs. Naidu, Amma doesn't work at your house at the end of the day. She works at Vimala Madam's house.

Vimala Madam's house is a problem.

It's a problem because Vimala Madam lives there.

My mother loves Vimala Madam, but I think she's creepy.

('Creepy' is a word that describes something that makes you feel shivery inside. You might feel that way because you are scared, or you might feel that way because you are disgusted. Creepy is kind of a little bit of both. I learned the word 'creepy' from a comic book I borrowed from Amir. This one was especially good because it had a ghost in it, but then the ghost turned out to be a person who was also a murderer. I'm sorry to give away the ending, Mrs. Naidu, but seeing as ~~you are dead~~ you don't go to bookstores any more, I thought maybe you wouldn't mind.)

So now, every day after school, I find something to do besides going to Vimala Madam's house. Which is why yesterday, I tried something new.

Yesterday, Annie Miss asked me if I wanted to come to a Child Rights Club meeting. I didn't know anything about child rights, but I did know that the club met for an hour, which meant that by the time it was over, Amma would be done with work, and I could go straight to our non-creepy home.

Miss brought biscuits – the good kind with chocolate in the middle. Deepti stayed too, and even though I didn't say anything, when she saw me, she took two biscuits, handed me one, and then sat down next to me, cross-legged on the floor. While we were nibbling, Miss told us that the purpose of the club would be to make sure that children like us could "recognize our rights." Apparently there's this really important thing called the Convention on the Rights of the Child. It's a list of stuff you should have if you're a child – which I am, because I am between the ages of six and fourteen. That part was kind of interesting since no one ever told me that I was allowed to have *anything*. Adults spend a lot more time on what kids are *not* allowed to do than what we *are*.

First on the list was education. Miss started talking about the Right to Education Act, which has a much longer name full of English words that I have never read in detective novels or comic books. I wrote them down so I can find out what they mean later. I guess a lot of other people don't know them either, because everyone calls the law 'RTE' for short.

Miss told us that RTE says that every private school in the country has to reserve seats for children under the age of 14 who are from 'economically weaker sections'. I don't exactly know what 'economically weaker sections' means, but I know that I belong to them, because that's what it says on all of the forms Amma fills out for my school.

"So let me get this straight," I said. "An economically weaker section kid can walk into any private school and they'll take her?"

(You may remember that I have a policy of not asking questions of adults. You can tell that I was excited because I broke this policy for the first time in a very, very, *very* long time.)

"Um," Miss said. "Yes. I mean, I think so. After the child submits some forms so that her fees can be covered by the government."

"Wait," I said. "This economically weak kid gets to go to the private school for free?"

"Yes," she said. "Or – actually, I'm not sure. It's free or a greatly reduced rate."

Do you know what this means, Mrs. Naidu?

Since you are a genius, you probably do. But just in case, let me present the clues again.

1. I am from an economically weaker section.
2. I am 12, which is between the ages of six and 14.
3. Kids between the ages of six and 14 who are economically weaker can go to private schools for free.
4. My best friend Amir goes to a private school.

Based on this evidence, Mrs. Naidu, I conclude that Amir and I can go to the same school.

Which maybe means that we can become best friends again.

I'm really glad I decided to try something new.

All the best,
Sarojini

July 4, 2013

Dear Mrs. Naidu,

This is our last assignment. It has been nice writing to you. I hope you won't miss my letters too much.

In this assignment, we are supposed to talk about our dreams for the future. I think that means talking about what we want to do when we grow up.

Usually when adults ask me about my future, I say that I like maths or pure sciences and that I'll study engineering or medicine.

But I only say that because that's what *all* adults want *all* kids to say.

(They never tell kids that's what they want, but it's *so* obvious.)

So here is a secret that I haven't told anyone, except for Amir. The secret is what I really want to be when I grow up. Are you ready?

A detective.

I know that it probably sounds odd, because it's not like there are any girl detectives (at least not in the books I've read) or even any Indian detectives (at least not that I've met – in books, it seems like they're mostly British, or sometimes American). But I want to be the first.

I don't want to be like Sherlock Holmes or anything, with that funny hat and that weird assistant. I want to be a respectable woman in a sari – probably a red or a pink sari, since Amma says that's best for dark skin like mine – who you can trust with all your most embarrassing problems. Everyone expects a detective to be a man, so if you're a woman, you can go undercover more easily, which means you can use the element of surprise. (In detective novels, the element of surprise is always extremely important.) Plus, I can't picture any man giving the laser-eyed look that my Amma gives, and I will definitely need that look when I stop murderers and thieves.

I am telling you this, Mrs. Naidu, because I think you know what it's like to do things that people don't think you should do. Like how you travelled all over the world by yourself and gave speeches about how women should vote and go to school, and some people didn't like that. It seems like they didn't like what you said and they didn't like that you left your husband and your children in India and travelled by yourself.

(I have to ask you, Mrs. Naidu – when you were in the UK, did you meet any detectives or spies? Were any of them Indian?)

Amma has lots of ideas about what my goals should be. Well, just one idea actually: Amma thinks I should become a lawyer.

Can you guess why?

The same reason she wants me to do everything: because of Vimala Madam.

Vimala Madam is a lawyer, but that is not the main thing about her. If you were paying attention, you'll remember that the main thing about her is that she is creepy. Not lawyerly. Creepy.

Her flat is dark and has all these teak doors and chairs and shelves that make you feel heavy inside. Then there are all these statues and pieces of art that look like they're expensive and that they'd shatter into a million tiny pieces if you breathed on them. And when she speaks to you – which she doesn't really ever do – she sounds more like she's barking than she's talking, probably because that's how you have to talk when you spend your whole life trying to get judges to listen to you. Plus, she does this crazy thing where she puts her glasses down her pointy nose and raises just one eyebrow, like everything you're saying is wrong, even if you're just saying hello.

Which is apparently what Amma thinks I ~~should~~ will do. Become a barking, eyebrow-raising, pointy-nosed lawyer.

Amma says that being a lawyer is the perfect job for me because I love reading so much. She says Vimala Madam reads all day too, which is why the house is full of books. You would think that a house full of books would be a good thing, but the books in Vimala Madam's house are not like the books I read, or the books you write – they're enormous and thick and dusty and boring. Amma also says that lawyers must make plenty of money because Vimala Madam has her own three-bedroom flat with a study and lots of hard-to-lift furniture and easy-to-break art. And she says that lawyers must be respected because Vimala Madam's photo comes in the newspaper all the time.

No offense, Mrs. Naidu, since I'm sure your photo was in the paper lots of times, but it isn't like you have to be respected to be on the front page. I mean, criminals are on the front pages all the time, aren't they? But when I said that to Amma, she said it was exactly that kind of logical thinking that would make me a good lawyer.

Then again, maybe not all lawyers are bad. Gandhi Thatha was a lawyer, wasn't he, Mrs. Naidu? And so was Panditji, I think. And so was Dr. Ambedkar. And you were friends with all of them, weren't you?

But then, it's one thing to be friends with a lawyer. It's an entirely different thing to *be* one.

All the best,
Sarojini

Dear Mrs. Naidu,

I know that the assignment is over, and that you probably have more important people to write letters to (even if they are ~~dead passed on~~ historical like you). But something happened today, Mrs. Naidu, and I want to talk about, but I can't, really – at least I can't with anyone I know. Except maybe you.

Remember how I told you about the Child Rights Clubmeeting? And how there is a law now that says that kids can go to private schools for free?

Well, Mrs. Naidu, when I heard that, I thought it was true.

Or actually, I *wanted* it to be true.

After the Child Rights Club meeting, I told Amma ~~exactly what I heard~~ what I thought I heard.

That I could go to any private school and they would let me enroll for free.

That they wouldn't charge us any fees but I could learn a lot and do well on my exams and then get a good job and then we could shift into a flat with running water and a real roof and maybe even a garden.

That maybe, if Amir and I were in the same school, we could be friends again.

Maybe even *best* friends again.

(As you've probably ~~guessed~~ concluded, Mrs. Naidu, I didn't tell Amma that last part. I just told her the part about learning and exams and a job and a new home.)

Amma didn't believe me at first, because it hadn't come in the Kannada language newspapers, which she reads every day at Vimala Madam's house.

But then she thought about it for a minute and said we should try anyway, because if we didn't try, then I definitely wouldn't get a seat. So she said we would go.

Mrs. Naidu, whenever you go to some place important like a private school, you need to take lots of forms. So before we left, Amma took out my birth certificate, our Below Poverty Line card, her voter ID, her income certificate, my injection card, my report card – pretty much every piece of paper we have with either of our names on it.

Amma wore her best sari, the cotton-silk one with the gold detail that one of her houses gave her because it's sort of frayed at the end. I pressed my uniform perfectly, forced every single one of my flyaway curls into neatly oiled braids, and shined my shoes for an extra-long time.

Then it was time to go.

I guess you're probably wondering where we went.

To be completely accurate, there are lots of private schools in Bangalore. But for me and Amma, there has always been just one: Greenhill Public School.

Greenhill Public is not as famous as some of Bangalore's other schools, like Baldwin's or Bishop Cotton's or St. Joseph's. But Vimala Madam sent her children there, and Vimala Madam has the best of everything, so Amma concluded that Greenhill must be the best.

Amma didn't ask me if I liked the school or anything, but I didn't mind. When I was in UKG, Vimala Madam's children still lived at home, and their Greenhill materials would just be lying around the house. I used to love flipping through the colourful pictures of birds and animals and plants in their science books, and the photos from all over the world in their social studies books. They always seemed to be studying the most interesting things – astronomy, kalamkari painting, Annie Besant, ghazals.

Plus Vimala Madam's kids won all these awards for things that I never knew anyone gave awards for, like writing the best poem, or running the fastest in the 500 metres, or participating in a talent show. I always thought awards were for things like exams and marks. I didn't think people could get awards for being fast or creative or just showing up.

In UKG, I couldn't wait to go to school, because I thought my school would be like Greenhill.

(If you've been paying attention, Mrs. Naidu, you know that Ambedkar School is nothing like Greenhill. In fact, it is the opposite of Greenhill.)

Which I guess is maybe the point Miss has been trying to make – school should make your brain *and* your heart happy.

But even if Greenhill *was* like Ambedkar School, it wouldn't matter. Greenhill is where Amir goes. So naturally, it's where I want to go too.

When we went through the front gate of Greenhill, all the colour and light and echoes made it hard to breathe. There were posters in English telling about clubs and activities. There were display cases full of art projects and photographs of students playing sports. It smelled like clean tiles and pencil shavings and fresh paper.

We didn't know who to speak to, so we went to the main office, where the walls were made of glass and there were lots of mirrors everywhere, like the inside of a jewellery store.

When we walked in, the secretary stared at us like we didn't belong.

When I saw her, I should've known that this was a bad idea. Everything about her was glittery and hard: the diamond in her nose, the zari border of her sari, the white of her hair. I should've asked Amma to take me back home.

But I didn't.

"Who are you?" the secretary asked in English.

When Amma and I just looked at each other, not knowing what to say, the woman repeated it in broken Kannada, "*Neevu yaaru?*"

"We are friends of Mrs. Vimala Rao," I blurted out in English, just so she knew we understood.

Amma looked surprise for a split second, but then her face went blank. "That's right," she said, in Kannada.

"*You* are friends with Vimala Rao?" the secretary asked. She was speaking Kannada too, but you could tell that she wasn't used to it – like she only used it when she was ordering people around, like her cook or the school ayah. "Vimala Rao the famous advocate?"

"Yes madam," I said, making my eyes look wide and innocent. "She's like a mother to me."

Okay, maybe that was a bit much.

You probably don't approve, Mrs. Naidu. But (no offense or anything), you probably never have to do anything to get someone to talk to you properly. I mean, if you wanted to speak to someone powerful, you could just say you were friends with Gandhiji. Who wouldn't want to talk to someone who was friends with Gandhiji?

Actually, you probably didn't even have to say that. You could just say you were Mrs. Sarojini Naidu, poetess, freedom fighter and former president of the Congress Party.

But Amma and I, we're not poetesses or presidents. We're just fighters.

At least, Amma is a fighter. I haven't decided what I am yet.

"Please Madam," Amma said, "can we see the headmistress?"

"What is this vital business that requires Madam's attention?" the secretary asked.

"We're here about the 25% reservations," I said in my most lawyerly voice.

The woman's eyebrows went up even further and her lips tightened.

"I'm from the economically weaker sections – see," I said, taking the pile of forms in Amma's hands and showing the secretary. "This is our BPL card. And our income certificate."

I was still trying to sound lawyerly, but I don't think lawyers' voices usually shake like mine did.

The woman held up her hand and smiled.

It was not the kind of smile that makes you feel better.

It was the kind of cold, rocky smile that tells you that you've just fallen into a trap that you set yourself.

"You're in, what?" she asked, "fifth standard?"

"Sixth," I said.

"Well," she said, crossing her arms and leaning backward, like she had just won something, "let me say this to you in plain language, so I'm sure you'll understand."

I felt Amma flinch. Under the table, I took her hand and squeezed it, hoping that would short circuit the lasers in her eyes.

"Here in Karnataka, RTE seats are for pre-nursery students only," the secretary said.

I looked at Amma and she looked at me. Annie Miss hadn't said anything like this, so I wasn't sure if it was true. But I didn't have proof either way, so I didn't say anything.

The secretary must've known, because she saw my face, and her smile glittered even more. "Sometimes we have extra seats in upper grades. Unfortunately I'm not sure that you would be eligible for them."

"Madam, my daughter's education is the most important thing in my life," Amma said. "Tell me what to do and I will do it."

"You see, the seats here at Greenhill are very much in demand," the secretary said, laughing breathily. "Securing a seat here requires… sacrifice."

She took out a piece of paper, wrote something down, folded it, and passed it to Amma, who picked it up before I could see it.

"Madam, we know that the fees are very expensive," I said, as my mother unfolded the paper. "That's why we came about the reservations."

"I've seen many income certificates like this," the

secretary said, ignoring me. "Most have cost the families several thousand rupees. Hardly any are accurate."

"What?" I asked.

Did she think we had made up Amma's income?

Why would anyone pretend to be poor when everyone knows it's better to be rich?

And what was on the piece of paper that Amma was now putting into her purse?

"Madam," my mother said, leaning across the desk. "Do you have children?" I saw the secretary's smile fade as Amma reached across the desk and took her hand. "I'm sure you do, and I'm sure you want the best for them. I'm sure you also want them to value honesty."

The secretary looked at Amma's rough, brown hand on top of her soft, fair one.

"At this time, Greenhill will not be able to offer your daughter a seat," she said, pulling away. She opened her drawer and picked up something that smelled like Dettol, and made a big show of rubbing it on her hands.

Amma had that look that she gets just before she tells off the corporation people who ignore our water problems or the men that come home drunk and wake everyone up or the boys who used to beat up Amir.

It was the look that she gets just before she says exactly what she needs to say to win a fight.

I waited, Mrs. Naidu, because I was sure that she would find the right words. She always finds the right words. Remember, I told you?

But this time, she didn't find the right words. She didn't use her laser eyes. She just stood up, and said, "Thank you for your time."

"Of course," the secretary answered.

That glittery smile.

Amma took my hand, and we left.

Or, actually, Amma took my hand and dragged me out of the school and out to the street and kept walking.

"Amma, what happened? Why didn't you say anything? Why did she think we were lying about our income certificate? Why are we walking when the bus is right there?"

You can tell how upset I was by the number of times I broke my no-questions-to-adults rule.

Amma only seemed to hear the last question, because she said, "I need some fresh air."

In Bangalore, the air is never fresh – especially on the main road. The world is never green and blue and the trees are never full of fruit and the frogs and the crickets are never louder than the traffic.

Today, though, one thing was louder than the traffic.

Above the screeching tyres and the honking horns and the mooing cows and the revving motorcycles,

I could hear the sound of Amma's heavy, angry breathing.

Mrs. Naidu, do you know what it feels like to hear your mother, who always has something say, being the kind of silent that is louder than words?

Do you know how it feels to know that you are the reason for it?

By the time we got home, it was almost dark. I swept the floor and Amma sat down to make dinner. After giving her a few minutes to take out her anger on the onions she was chopping – or, actually, slashing into tiny pieces – I said, "Amma, I'm sorry."

I thought those were the right words. But they weren't.

Amma turned to me and asked, "What for?"

Wasn't it obvious?

"I'm sorry I made you go there and talk to that woman," I said. "I'm sorry I tried to leave my school. It's fine. My school is fine. I shouldn't have wanted to change."

My mother took a deep breath, and I thought she was going to scream. Instead, she spoke in a low voice, a voice that was calm the way a pot of water is just before it boils – smooth on the surface, but steaming like it was about to bubble and roll.

"Never apologize for wanting something," she said. "Just find another way."

Mrs. Naidu, it seems like what you wanted more than anything was freedom for India. And thank you for wanting that, because you got what you wanted, and because of that I am free.

But did you ever hurt someone you loved because of what you wanted?

Right now, wanting something doesn't feel so great.

Maybe it's better not to want anything at all.

All the best,
Sarojini

Dear Mrs. Naidu,

Before I read this book about you, I never knew how much you travelled. You went to cities that I don't even know how to pronounce – Cincinnati, Aden, Dar es Salaam, Nairobi, Chicago. And it seems like in all of these cities, you got to meet a lot of people at speeches and dinners and meetings about political issues. Some of those people became your friends.

When you went back home, did you wonder if you would ever see those friends again?

Did you ever think about the friends you were leaving behind?

Even though the place I live is not a faraway country, it *is* a place where people leave all the time. Like my friend Madhumita, who taught me how to play gili danda in Class Two. She left because her Appa started drinking so her Amma took her back to their village to get away.

Or like my neighbour, Yashoda, who used to plait my hair in the mornings and walk me to school when Amma had to leave for work early. She left because she got married and moved to the neighbourhood where her husband lived.

Or like my Appa, who disappeared when I was a baby. I don't know why he left. He just did.

Amir and his family weren't like that.

Amir and his family were supposed to stay.

But they didn't.

I saw Amir yesterday at pretty much the worst possible time. The water truck had just come and I was filling up some plastic drums and hauling them back home.

(Amma started at two new houses, and so now I have to get the water every day, instead of just sometimes. When it comes to fetching the water, 'sometimes' is better than 'always'.)

I ended up standing next to Hema Aunty, who normally talks to the other aunties, but today she decided to talk to me.

"Who was that girl I saw you with the other day?" Hema Aunty asked me. "That dirty little thing without shoes." She said it extra loudly, and Nimisha Aunty, who was standing behind her, started giggling.

"Deepti's not dirty, Aunty," I said. "She bathes every day at the construction site."

"She lives at the construction site?" Hema Aunty clicked her teeth and shook her head. "Don't associate with her, darling. You're such a nice girl. You know how those construction people are. They come from these backwards places with their backwards ideas. Your Deepti will be married with three children in a year."

That made me angry, Mrs. Naidu, because even though I've barely even spoken to Deepti, I don't think she's like that. But I couldn't be too angry, because when I first met Deepti, I thought those same things. Now that I see her in class every day, though, I can tell that she's smart, and that she's not mean or impolite or anything. She's just what my Amma would call a little bit 'rough and ready.'

So instead of telling Hema Aunty she was wrong, which I probably should've done, I said, "I should go before I'm late for school, Aunty."

"Hmmph," Hema Aunty snorted. As I was leaving, she turned to Nimisha Aunty and said, "Bad enough she was always with that Muslim boy. Now this. But what do you expect from a girl with no father?"

After I heard that, I had trouble keeping my balance, partly because my eyes were misty and my stomach was tight, and partly because the drum was so heavy and the ground was so wet from last night's rains.

Right at that moment, Amir came up on his bicycle, which was new, wearing his fancy uniform, which was also new.

Like I said, pretty much the worst possible time.

"Hey, Saru," he said, parking his bike.

"Hi Amir," I said, putting the drum down. (Which, by the way, everyone knows you should never do, because then you have to squeeze your feet into the mud and bend your knees and arch your back and pick the whole heavy thing back up again.)

"Want me to get that?" he asked.

"No thanks," I said, looking at the stiff collar of his shirt and the pleats in his pants and thinking that the fastest way to Greenhill was definitely not through our neighbourhood.

"But aren't you going to be late?" he asked.

I shrugged. Wanting to change the subject, I asked, "How's school?"

"It's okay," he said. "We have this cricket field and all new equipment. Plus we have art class and I'm learning how to paint."

"That's good," I said. But only because I didn't know what else to say.

"How's our – um, how's Ambedkar School?"

"There's a new teacher and she started this Child Rights Club," I said.

"Are you going so you don't have to go to Vimala Madam's house?"

"Actually, yes," I said, laughing. He laughed too.

"Hey, this is for you," Amir said, and handed me a heavy-ish plastic bag.

I looked inside. Then I looked at Amir.

"It's a backpack full of school supplies," he said.

"There's those pencils you like – the red kind with the stripes? Plus there's chart paper and everything."

"Why does it have your brother's company name on it?" I asked, looking at the logo on the front.

"They were doing donations for government school students," Amir said. "And you're a government school student, so, I thought maybe…"

Mrs. Naidu, I should've been grateful. Amma and I never have enough money for all the supplies I need, and normally I buy whatever I can and then get the rest from school, even though I know the teachers buy the 'extra supplies' for us with their own money. Amir knew it was hard for us, and he was just trying to help me.

But do you know how it feels to have your best friend remind you that you go to a government school and he doesn't?

Do you know how it feels to have him ride up on his shiny new bicycle with his shiny new uniform and hand you a donation from a charity while you're standing in an extremely un-shiny, un-new nightie with mud on your bare feet?

No matter how I was feeling, I still had to get the drum of water home before I changed into my uniform and plaited my hair and went to my government school that didn't have any sports equipment or cricket fields or art rooms. I took the cover off and put the new backpack on my shoulders and then I stretched my arms a little bit and bent my knees and hitched the drum up on my hip. My whole body ached.

I guess he could see how hard it was for me, because he said, "Why don't I carry that for you, Saru?"

And then he said, "It'll be just like the old days."

That was what did it, Mrs. Naidu. More than the bicycle or the bag or anything else.

It was like Amir was drawing a line in our friendship and separating it into two halves.

There was our old friendship, when we were equal – so equal that we shared the same roof. And then there was this new friendship which, lately, didn't seem like a friendship at all.

So I said, "I don't need help."

And then I added, "Not from you."

Mrs. Naidu, you know that expression they use in books a lot, the one that goes, "he looked like he'd just been slapped"?

Well, this isn't something I like to talk about, but I've seen Amir after he's just been slapped.

I know what he looks like.

And Mrs. Naidu, when I said those things to Amir, those things I shouldn't have said? The look on his face was so, so, much worse.

I probably could've apologized, taken it back. But I was so mad, Mrs. Naidu, so mad about everything.

About having to carry water through the unpaved alleyways.

About having to change into my scratchy, thin uniform.

About being the kind of person who might not be poor enough to go to Greenhill Public as a reservations student, but is definitely poor enough to lose a best friend.

So instead of apologizing, I turned around and left.

So I wouldn't have to see how much I hurt my friend.

So he wouldn't have to see how much he hurt me.

So both of us wouldn't have to admit that when Amir moved away, he left more than just a tin roof behind.

All the best,
Sarojini

Dear Mrs. Naidu,

I know I said I was done wanting things. But no matter how hard I try, Mrs. Naidu, the wanting keeps coming back.

When I walk across Ambedkar's pebbly compound I wish I was walking through Greenhill's shiny tiled hallways. When I sit on the floor in my classroom I wish I was sitting at the rows of desks and benches at Greenhill with cubbyholes where you could store notebooks and pencils. When my teacher passes out the same story books we've been reading over and over again since Class Three I wish I could choose something from the stuffed shelves in the Greenhill library.

Then, on top of all of that, when I was leaving this afternoon, Annie Miss stopped me.

"Come, Sarojini. We have Child Rights Club," she said.

I was about to make an excuse, but then I remembered that if I didn't stay, I'd have to go to Vimala Madam's house.

So I shrugged and followed Miss out of the grey July breeze and into the stuffy classroom where the air was thick and still because the power had gone and the fan hadn't run all day.

I bet Greenhill has a generator.

"Welcome everyone," Miss said. I looked around. By 'everyone' she meant five of us – which, to be fair, was two more than last time, so I guess it was kind of an improvement.

"Miss, biscuits?" Roshan asked from the back of the room.

"Not today, Roshan," Miss said.

Roshan and his two friends left, so it was just me and Deepti. Which was one less than last time.

I started to feel bad for Miss, until I remembered what she had done to me. Not on purpose, but still.

"Sarojini, you raised some good questions during our last meeting," Miss said, opening her bag.

(Which I wasn't expecting, Mrs. Naidu, because you know how adults are with questions. Maybe Miss thinks questions are good for our hearts.)

"I brought some copies of the law," Miss said. "I thought we could look at it together."

"Oh," I said. I probably should've been grateful or something.

"Here is a version in Kannada," she said, passing out a glossy pamphlet with a drawing of a fair girl with brown plaits on the front. "Now remember, children, this law is designed for you. Well, for us, actually. Using the law, teachers and students can work together to realize the right to education for all."

Miss sounded awkward, like she was repeating something she had mugged up from one of her just-and-beautiful-world books, but couldn't quite remember properly. Still, in a way, it made me feel hopeful, like she cared enough to look for information about the stuff she didn't know. I started to feel a little less angry.

"Let's start with the reservations section, since that's what you asked about, Sarojini," she said. "According to this document, you can only register in the first accepting grades of a school. So that would be LKG or UKG, or sometimes Class One."

If only she had said that a week ago.

"My cousin in Pune is in Sixth, and she just got a seat," said Deepti.

"That can't be," Miss said. "This document clearly says that it's only early grades where there are admissions."

Deepti shrugged, so Miss kept going.

"It also says that there are some private schools that are exempt from the requirement," she said. "That means that they don't have to admit more students because they have so many minority students already. Like, for example, if there is a school for orphans, they are already serving the economically needy, so they wouldn't have to take in more students."

"But a lot of the private schools use that to keep us out," Deepti said. "I tried to get my brother into UKG at St. Augustina. The school said they were Christian so they didn't have to do reservations, but most of the students I saw there were definitely Hindu. I mean, maybe they just said that because I went without my Amma and Appa, but either way, it doesn't seem fair."

Are you surprised to hear this, Mrs. Naidu?

No, no, not the part about the school keeping Deepti's brother out – that's not surprising.

I mean the part where Deepti, with her grey-but-used-to-be-purple pavade and her dusty feet and her twiggy arms marched into one of the poshest schools in Bangalore and asked if her brother could get admission.

What I did was crazy, Mrs. Naidu, but what Deepti did? That was *much* crazier.

"Why would they want to keep your brother or any other child from realizing their rights?" Miss asked. But then she giggled nervously, and I could tell she wasn't sure what she was saying.

"They think we're a bad influence," Deepti said.

"Why?" I asked, even though I maybe thought the same thing.

"Because we're poor," Deepti shrugged. "They think we're dirty and badly behaved."

That should probably have made me think about Deepti spitting, Mrs. Naidu, but it didn't. You know what I thought about instead?

How the secretary at Greenhill had put that smelly stuff on her hand after she pulled away from Amma.

I wondered what it would be like to go to school in a place like that. A place where everyone thought they were better than you, and where parents thought that you were rude and carried diseases just because your Amma made less money than they did.

"I'm sorry you feel that way, Deepti," Miss said. "But the government passed this law so that it could help students like you. The government of this country believes in you and wants you to succeed."

"If they really want us to succeed," Deepti said, "why don't they just fix the schools we can go to for free?"

This really stopped me, Mrs. Naidu. My whole life I've been sure that government schools were rubbish. I mean, obviously something you pay for is better than something that's free, right?

But then I thought about what Deepti said and realized that maybe I was wrong.

Because I thought about you, Mrs. Naidu.

I thought about how you fought so hard for women's rights to education.

I thought about how you once said, "the hand that rocks the cradle is the power that rules the world."

When you said that, I don't think you were thinking about the girls who go to Greenhill. I think you were thinking about girls like me and Deepti who could never afford to go to a fancy school.

So why would a law about the Right to Education talk so much about private schools instead of the schools we already go to?

"Actually," Miss said, flipping through the glossy pamphlet, "I think most of this law is about government schools."

"What does it say?" Deepti asked.

"I don't know," said Miss, looking anxious. Then she kind of lit up. "I have a wonderful idea. Let's read it together! There's no reason that a teacher has to tell you all the information all the time. This is an opportunity for us to learn side by side."

If any other teacher had said that, I would've thought she was being lazy, Mrs. Naidu. But I think Miss really believes that reading the law together would be a good experience.

The only good thing about Child Rights Club,

Mrs. Naidu, was that it went late enough that I knew Amma would be home. One less Vimala Madam day for me!

All the best,
Sarojini

July 12, 2013

Dear Mrs. Naidu,

I'm sorry to be bothering you so much, Mrs. Naidu. I mean, for one thing, the assignment is over, and for another thing, you ~~are passed away no longer with us~~ have better things to do than read my letters. But I was reading the book about you and I read this part about how you were in a protest once and the police came. Everyone ran away, except for you. Apparently you were waiting so long that you asked someone to bring a rocking chair to the verandah. You sat in the chair and just rocked and rocked and rocked until the Britishers came and put you in jail.

How did you get so much courage, Mrs. Naidu?

I thought if you wouldn't mind telling me, maybe I could get some too.

This morning, I stopped by the construction site on the way to school. Deepti's been borrowing pencils and erasers from other students, so I figured she probably needed a backpack and supplies. As you know, Mrs. Naidu, I happened to have some extras this year.

When I handed the backpack to her, Deepti said, "Thanks," which is what I probably should have said to the person who gave it to me in the first place.

(We all know what I did instead, so there's really no need to bring it up now.)

"How's your brother?" I asked.

"Abhi? He seems happy," she said. "He's been singing this rhyme over and over again, about an elephant or something. He even makes an elephant noise. It's cute, when it's not annoying."

"So... you tried to get him into St. Augustina?" I asked.

Deepti rolled her eyes, which I guess was her way of saying yes.

"I tried to get into Greenhill Public," I said. "I mean, I didn't know about the nursery school rule, so I tried to get myself a seat."

"Really?" said Deepti. I'm not sure, Mrs. Naidu, but I think maybe she was impressed.

"Yeah," I said. "They made me feel so small."

"Well, of course," Deepti said, like I'd said the most obvious thing in the world. "I feel small even standing across the street from that place. I can't believe you went inside! Wow."

On the outside I shrugged, but on the inside I felt a million times bigger.

"They said no, and I didn't know what to do," I said. "They knew all the rules and I didn't."

"That's why we have to *learn* the rules," Deepti

said. "Miss is nice, and she'll help us, but she doesn't know how this stuff works. What we really need is someone who can explain the law to us."

Mrs. Naidu, when you were sitting on that rocking chair, waiting to go to jail, and then the police finally came, and you knew what you had to do, did you feel really scared and really brave at the same time? Because that's how I felt right then.

The scared part was my stomach twisting, like it does before I do something I don't want to do.

The brave part was my heart speeding up, like something big was about to happen, and I was ready for it.

I took a deep breath and said, "I know someone"

I know only one lawyer, Mrs. Naidu. I think you know who she is.

Wish me luck, Mrs. Naidu. If I don't write to you for a few days, ask Amma to check in the walls behind Vimala Madam's library. That's where murderers who are also evil geniuses always hide their victims.

All the best,
Sarojini

July 15, 2013

Dear Mrs. Naidu,

There are a lot of bad things about having to wait for the water truck every day before school. I'm late a lot. My back always hurts and my clothes always get dirty. I sometimes see people I don't want to see.

(If you've been paying attention, Mrs. Naidu, you know who I'm talking about. I'm glad that you're a genius and can figure it out, because I really don't want to remind you.)

There is one good thing about the water truck, though. People talk. And if you are in the right place at the right time, you hear things.

Useful things.

Like this morning, for example. I went to the truck and I saw Deepti. I stood next to her as we elbowed our way to the front to fill our jugs.

"I'm going to be late for school again," I said.

"I'm not sure if I'll even *get* to school," Deepti sighed. "I still have to give Abhi a bath. By the time that's done, the morning will be gone!"

"But the English teacher is always late," I pointed out. "She won't even know you're missing. In fact, she'll think you're early."

Deepti laughed, and she said, "Good point. Plus she never combs her hair properly, does she? If I show up with my hair half plaited, I can just tell her that I'll do her hair if she'll do mine!"

I pictured Deepti braiding Miss's hair, and I giggled. It felt good to have a friend to laugh with at the water truck ~~just like when Amir used to come with me~~. Deepti couldn't lift my drums for me, but at least she could lift my spirits.

Deepti elbowed me, and I thought maybe she was trying to get me out of the way. Then she tilted her head and raised her eyebrows, and I realized that she wanted me to listen to Hema Aunty, who was complaining.

Normally, that's nothing special. Honestly, Mrs. Naidu, Hema Aunty complains so much that usually I don't pay any attention. She complains about everything: mosquitos, heat, cold, her children, her neighbours, her house, her husband, even her own face. But when I listened, I realized why Deepti had elbowed me. Today, Hema Aunty was complaining about something important.

"I took my Roshan there to that Gerao-something school – what is it called?" she was saying.

"The one by the big church?" Kamala Aunty asked. "Geronimo School?"

"That one!" Hema Aunty said. "So I said to the headmistress, someone told me that you have 25%

reservations for economically weaker sections and backward castes. I am economically weak, I told her. I am backward caste. And, you know, my Roshan talks back and he is lazy as anything, but he is sharp."

"Wow, she said something nice about her son!" Deepti whispered to me. I giggled, because Deepti's only been coming to the truck for a few days and she's already figured everyone out.

"Then this headmistress, can you believe her? She said to me, that'll be twenty thousand rupees." Hema Aunty did that thing aunties do where they touch their foreheads and then fling their arms out, like they're casting off drishti or something. It's what they do right before they turn red and start threatening to have a heart attack. "Can you imagine? This is supposed to be a government program and these people are asking me to pay for a seat."

"Twenty thousand? That's nothing," said Mary Aunty. "I tried to get a seat for Joseph, and they wanted me to pay a full thirty thousand. And that was only if he passed some entrance exam. Twenty thousand is a bargain."

"How can they do that?" Deepti asked. "Doesn't the law say they have to make it free?"

"Law? What law?" Mary Aunty said, sucking her teeth. "Since when did the law apply to people like us? Whenever we decide to go get something we're entitled to, there is a line of people waiting to take our money. Even getting that BEO to sign some useless form cost me."

"What's a BEO?" Deepti asked.

(You might have noticed, Mrs. Naidu, that Deepti's asking-adults-questions policy is the opposite of mine.)

"Block Education Officer," Amina Aunty answered. "These people had no money before. What bribes could you get for a government school, na? But now this reservations business has come in and they've seen their opportunity."

"It's enough to make my blood pressure shoot up," Hema Aunty said, fanning herself with the pallu of her sari. "It will kill me, I tell you."

Hema Aunty has always loved drama, so don't worry, Mrs. Naidu, she wasn't in any danger. But I understood why she was angry. I think my blood pressure rose too.

"If you ask me, these reservations are a waste of time," Amina Aunty said.

"Completely useless!" Nimisha Aunty agreed. "This new law says we're supposed to get a free education. So why should people charge us? And how are we supposed to make money if we don't have jobs because we don't have schooling ourselves?"

"God only knows," Kamala Aunty said, looking at the sky. The other women nodded too and touched their foreheads and their hearts and muttered, "Jai Ram," all except Amina Aunty, who said something about Allah.

"What to do? It is written," Hema Aunty said. "Women have to bear the burden of life. Mothers more than daughters. Daughters more than sons."

Deepti and I had filled our drums by then, so we left together.

"I don't care what's written," she said - though it sounded more like a growl. "I'm rewriting it."

Mrs. Naidu, I think Deepti's a lot like you – she's a fighter. And she doesn't let other people distract her or make her doubt herself. Plus, she's kind of a writer – she doesn't write poems like you do, but she writes her own destiny.

(I'm not sure who is writing my destiny, Mrs. Naidu, but probably someone pretty boring, since nothing exciting ever happens to me.)

"When are you meeting that lawyer madam?" Deepti asked me.

"After school one day," I said. "Do you want to come?"

"I have to watch my brother," she said, shaking her head. "You'll have to go alone."

"Do you think this law can really help us?"

"I don't know. But that's what laws are supposed to do, right?"

She has a point, Mrs. Naidu. I know you believed

in laws – that's why you were so involved in the government that formed when India first became free, and why you became a governor. You changed things using laws and government. Maybe Deepti and I can too.

We walked back to our area without saying anything.

Mrs. Naidu, you know how silences can sometimes be loud? Like they're full of questions and doubts and tension?

This wasn't that kind of silence.

This is the kind of silence that is quiet with all the questions you're saving up to ask each other, because someday, when you know each other better, there won't be room for silence. There will be too many other sounds to make.

All the best,
Sarojini

July 17, 2013

Dear Mrs. Naidu,

I did it. I spoke to Vimala Madam. And you know what? It wasn't so bad!

I went there after school, even though I really didn't want to. I wasn't thinking about the law or the questions I was going to ask or what I was going to say, like I should have been. I was thinking about all kinds of other things instead. Like, for example, whether Amir was angry at me and whether Deepti and I could become better friends and whether the only way to get seats was to buy them. And then I thought about how maybe if we understood the law, Deepti and I could both get seats at Amir's school, and how maybe the three of us could be friends.

Anyway, after all that thinking, I got to Vimala Madam's house and Amma answered the door and told me that Madam was expecting me.

(I asked Amma if it was okay for me to ask Vimala Madam about a school project. Which, if you remember, Mrs. Naidu, is the best way to get an adult to let you do what you want.)

(I know it's not completely honest. But it's *mostly* honest, right?)

Amma said I should knock on the door and reminded me to be polite and not take up too much of Madam's time. Then she fixed my skirt and patted down my hair and wiped something off my cheek even though there was probably nothing there, and then she kind of nodded and shoved me towards the study in the back of the flat.

Let me tell you, Mrs. Naidu, if I was scared before I was even more scared now – although I was also curious. I've been in Vimala Madam's home so many times but I've never been in that study. When she's in there, she makes all kinds of scary noises. I hear her on the phone yelling, and I hear thumping a lot, like she's getting huge, heavy books off the shelves, books that might be full of laws but also might be full of recipes for boiling children.

(I know, Mrs. Naidu, you probably don't approve of me describing Vimala Madam this way, like she's an evil genius in a detective novel. But you have to understand that everything about her is different than any other woman I've ever met. And don't say you're like that, Mrs. Naidu, because I'm reading about you and all the things you've done, and I don't think you were evil – I think you were just a genius.)

I needed courage then, Mrs. Naidu. So you know what I did?

I thought of how Amir might need help in English.

I thought of how Deepti was so smart but kept switching schools.

I thought of how the secretary woman treated Amma like she was lower than dirt.

And then I thought of you asking for a rocking chair before the Britishers took you to jail.

Then I swallowed really hard, like I was swallowing down all the doubts and fear and nerves, and knocked on that huge, heavy door.

"Is that you, Sarojini?" came a voice.

"Yes," I said, through all those layers of wood and money and evil.

"Come," she said.

When I walked in, Vimala Madam was sitting at a desk and looking at a thick book. She was wearing a modern kurta, like the kind you get at the stores on 100 feet road, and baggy salwars, no dupatta. Her thick white hair puffed around her face in frizzy tangles, the way mine does when I keep running my fingers through it while I'm taking exams. When she saw me, she cleared her throat, and said, "Your mother tells me you need help on a school project."

"Yes, Madam," I said, launching into the speech I had rehearsed with Amma. "Thank you for your time, Madam. I know you're very busy, Madam, and–"

"Don't apologize so much," she interrupted.

Which was funny, Mrs. Naidu, because Amma told me the same thing just a couple of nights ago.

"Okay, I'm sorry," I said. "I mean, I'm not sorry. I mean, I'm sorry I said I'm sorry, but –"

"What do you need help with, Sarojini?" she barked.

(You see what I'm talking about, Mrs. Naidu?)

"I need help understanding a law," I said.

Then she did that thing, Mrs. Naidu. The thing I told you about, remember? Where she puts her glasses down her nose and then raises just one eyebrow.

"The Right to Free and Compulsory Education Act of 2009," I said, carefully reciting the long and complicated English syllables I had memorized this afternoon, and reaching into my backpack and pulling out the pamphlet Annie Miss gave us at the Child Rights Club meeting. "I need to know what it says." When she kept staring me, I nudged it across the desk, and added, "Please, Madam, if you don't mind."

She stared at me with her eyebrow and her glasses and her hair. Then she cleared her throat, crossed her arms, and leaned back in her chair, pushing her glasses onto the top of her head. Her eyebrow was still up. She didn't touch the pamphlet.

Let me tell you, Mrs. Naidu, the glasses-on-the-head thing was much worse than the glasses-on-the-nose thing.

"When young lawyers come to me with questions

about laws," Vimala Madam said, "they usually do so for a reason."

She paused, like I was supposed to talk. But I didn't know what to say.

"As in," she said, "they think that this particular law can help them. Perhaps they are trying to defend a client, or to convince a judge to consider a new angle to a case. They come to me asking what the law can do and how it can help them."

She paused again, but I still didn't know what she meant. I wasn't a lawyer. I was a twelve-year-old government school student, which is probably the opposite of a lawyer.

She knew that, right?

"What I am asking you, Sarojini, is this: how do you think this law can help you?"

Well, why didn't she just say so?

"This law says that private schools have to let me in because I'm from the economically weaker sections," I said. "At least, someone told me that it says that. I want to know for sure."

"I see," Vimala Madam said. "And why does this interest you?"

"I go to a government school," I said. After a minute, when she kept staring me, I added, "But I *want* to go to a good school."

"Why do you want to go to a good school, exactly?" she asked.

What kind of an adult asks a kid a question like that?

An evil genius adult. That's what kind.

"I want to pass Tenth and then go to higher studies," I said.

"Why is that?" Vimala Madam asked again.

"I want to get a job with a good salary. I want to move Amma to our own home," I said. "I want Amma to be proud of me and to be able to stop cleaning houses and to rest."

I don't think I've ever said "I want" so many times in my life.

(There was one more *I want*, Mrs. Naidu, but I didn't say it out loud.)

When I was done, Madam stared at me. Honestly, I wasn't sure if that meant she was going to help or that she was going to fry me with some evil genius instrument in her office.

Finally, she said, "Give."

I stood across the wide table while she picked up the law and put her glasses back down over her eyes – which is where they belong, so I don't know why she ever moves them. She looked at the law for just a second before she looked up at me.

"This is in Kannada," she said.

I nodded.

"You read Kannada well," she said.

"Better than English," I admitted.

"Then come over here," she said. "And bring a chair."

So I got a metal chair from the other side of the room and unfolded it next to her. She put the pamphlet between us, like Amir and I used to do when we wanted to read the same comic book. Then she turned to Section 12, which is the part of the law about reservations for economically weaker sections.

And from there, things got to be not so bad, Mrs. Naidu.

In fact, they got to be pretty great.

Vimala Madam didn't speak to me like a teacher. She didn't act like she was smarter than me, even though I think she probably is.

She talked to me more like we were both adults who knew stuff, and could figure things out together.

It made me feel like a grown up.

Like a lawyer.

I learned how the Block Education Officer is supposed to help me and Amma use the reservations to get into area private schools. And how in Karnataka, the schools admit in Class One or Upper KG or whatever the first grade of the school is, but that they can give seats to students like me if they can't fill their 25% in the lower grades. (Other states admit students in all grades, which explains Deepti's cousin in Pune.) And how a lot of private schools in Bangalore are calling themselves 'minority institutions' so they don't have to take in students like me.

(A lot of this isn't in the pamphlet, but Vimala Madam just knows about it because she's a human rights lawyer.)

(Don't tell Amma, Mrs. Naidu, but after this, I think being a lawyer might not be so bad.)

When we finished, I felt hopeful because I knew the rules. But then at the same time, I knew it was going to be really hard. Especially for me and Deepti together. I didn't want to take a seat if she didn't get one, and I definitely didn't want her to get a seat without me.

"Let me ask you something, Sarojini," Vimala Madam said. "Now we've been through Section 12, would you like to know what is in the rest of the law?"

"Whatever you think is best, Madam," I said.

"Let's go back to your reason for wanting to know about RTE. Tell me again why you came to me."

"So I could go to a private school."

"Well, yes," she said. Her eyebrow went up again, which made me realize I hadn't taken the time to appreciate when it was down. "But what was your reason for going to a private school?"

"To get a good education," I said.

"Correct," Vimala Madam said, nodding. "To get a good education. NOT to go to a private school."

"But… if I don't go to a private school how will I get a good education?"

"Why, at the school you already go to!" she said.

"But Madam," I said, thinking maybe she had forgotten. "Remember, I told you I go to a government school?"

"Exactly right," she said. And she looked so pleased that I didn't want to tell her that I had no idea what she was talking about.

Please don't be offended by this, Mrs. Naidu, because I know I'm young and haven't done anything that you've done and still have a lot to learn. But when I started going through the law with Vimala Madam, I started to feel like I think you must've felt when you and Gandhiji and Panditji and Ambedkarji and everybody else realized that they had found the way to get rid of the Britishers for good, and that it was going to work.

It was like I was discovering all of this power that I have, even though I'm just a twelve-year-old girl.

Did you know that our teachers are not allowed to hit us? Hitting is called 'corporal punishment,' and it's illegal in India.

Did you know that every single school in India is supposed to have certain facilities? There's a list at the back of the law. It has all the required things like toilets for boys and girls and drinking water and playgrounds. *Playgrounds*, Mrs. Naidu. Abhi would love that.

Also, did you know that every school should have a school management committee that has parents and teachers on it that is supposed to manage the budget and help improve the building? Vimala Madam said students can join too. Annie Miss would love that.

When Amma knocked at the door, I don't know who was more surprised, me or her. Me, because the time had gone so quickly, or her, because Madam and I were leaning so close together we were almost on top of each other, and we were laughing and talking and I was getting really excited.

"Well, Sarojini, it was a pleasure," Madam said, shaking my hand.

"Um, thank – thank you, Madam," I said. No one had ever shaken my hand before. At least no one like Vimala Madam.

"Now, my dear, I am going to give you a task," she told me, closing the pamphlet and handing it to me.

"Yes?" I said, tucking it into my backpack.

"You must share what you have learned with your fellow students. Then you must come back and tell me what they think."

"Okay," I said, nodding.

"Okay-ah?" Amma said loudly.

"Sorry, I mean, yes Madam," I said, blushing. "Of course, Madam. Thank you, Madam."

Vimala Madam looked from me to Amma and back to me. Then she burst out laughing.

But it didn't feel mean. It felt good. Like something had changed between the two of us. Or maybe even the three of us, because even Amma smiled a little bit.

Not the way things have changed between me and Amir, though.

This was a change for the better.

All the best,
Sarojini

July 20, 2013

Dear Mrs. Naidu,

I know it's only been a couple of days since I wrote to you, but a lot has happened. I guess maybe that's how your life was too – everything was the same for a long time, and then all of a sudden, everything changed. Maybe you kept trying and trying to get the Britishers to leave, and they wouldn't go, and so you thought you would spend your whole life fighting. But then one day, they finally left, and it was what you wanted, but then everything was different.

(To be clear, this change that I'm talking about isn't as big as the Britishers Quitting India, Mrs. Naidu. Just so you don't get too excited or anything.)

Anyway, today was Saturday, and I only had a half day of school, and I finished my chores and my homework and everything, so Amma said it was okay if I went to see Deepti at the construction site. I had seen her in school but we hadn't had a chance to talk about what I learned, about how to get private school seats.

I was so excited, Mrs. Naidu. On the way, I practiced my Vimala Madam impression, especially the eyebrow part.

(No story is ever complete without an evil genius. Just ask any detective.)

Which is probably why I forgot to take the long way to Deepti's house, past the used paper shop and the hospital and then around the luxury apartments to the construction site. My feet just took me the way they've been going for years – through the coconut grove, under the overpass, and onto the main road.

Which is the road the call centre is on.

Which is the place where Farooq works.

Which I passed at exactly the time when the workers get their tea break.

Which is why I heard a voice yelling, "Sarojini!" even after I realized where I was and tried to duck back into the grove before someone noticed me.

Slowly, I turned and said, "Hello, bhaiyya."

"Hi there, chotti," Farooq said. He had a big smile on his face. In one hand, he held a steaming paper cup. In the other, he held a metal flask that I knew was full of Tasmiah Aunty's chai. My mouth started watering.

"Do you want some?" he said, like he could read my mind. Which he probably can, Mrs. Naidu. We've known each other that long.

"It's okay, bhaiyya," I lied, "I just had tiffin. Thanks."

"So late?" he said, and poured me a cup anyway.

"I don't think Aunty would let you sleep that much. Have some."

Mrs. Naidu, do you know what it's like to have something you love after a long, long time? Something you've been craving that you didn't even know you missed?

That chai tasted like cardamom and ginger and friendship and love.

It tasted so good that I had to close my eyes, because I wasn't sure what would happen if I didn't.

Farooq noticed – because he notices everything– and laughed.

And then I felt kind of silly and I laughed too, which meant I could open my eyes again, and I could say, "Thanks, bhaiyya. I missed this chai. Please tell Aunty."

"Of course," Farooq said. "We miss you too, Saru."

If you'll notice, Mrs. Naidu, I didn't say anything about missing anybody. I just said I missed the chai.

But that's Farooq for you.

"You haven't come by lately, chotti," Farooq said. I opened my mouth to give an excuse, but before I could, he said, "Wait, don't tell me – you've finished all the detective stories at Gangarams?"

I couldn't help it, Mrs. Naidu. I smiled again. It's funny, because when I see my classmates at school with their older brothers I am really glad I'm an only child. But whenever I see Farooq or Tariq, I kind of wish I had siblings.

"No," I said. "I've just been busy. Our new teacher is very strict."

"Strict?" Farooq asks. His body got all stiff. "Does she hit you?"

"No," I said slowly, because I hadn't thought about it before. "Actually, she doesn't."

"Then strict how?"

"Strict like she gives a lot of work. Mostly she gives us books and stories and then wants to know our opinions. She keeps telling us she wants our hearts *and* our brains to grow. I don't even know what that means, except it must have something to do with extra work, because she gives twice as many assignments as Geetha Miss gave us last year."

"Wow," Farooq said, almost to himself. "Not bad."

He kind of stared off into space, and it was the perfect time for me to ask the question that was hanging in the air between us, the question about how Amir was doing and whether maybe he and I were still friends.

But you know how grown ups are about questions, Mrs. Naidu.

Not that Farooq is a grown up, exactly. But now with his flask and his job and everything, he's not a kid anymore, either.

So instead I said, "Um."

I guess that made him remember I was here, because he looked down at me and said, "You know, you can still come over sometimes. Amir could use a friend."

"I thought he'd probably have a lot of friends at his new school," I said out loud. The part I didn't say out loud was, *I thought he probably doesn't want to be friends with me anymore.*

"Actually," Farooq said, "I don't think he has any friends at all."

"I've seen him with lots of other boys," I said, "walking home from school."

"He doesn't walk with them anymore," Farooq said. "He just did that the first week or so. Lately, I haven't seen him with anyone at all."

Then I started to worry.

Because I started to remember.

I remembered how at Ambedkar School, the kids in our class used to make fun of Amir for being kind of small and hanging out with girls like me, and how the older kids in our neighbourhood used to get angry at him for speaking Urdu at home, and how his brothers and I were always sticking up for him because he was never very good at fighting.

(But do private school kids fight? Isn't that just something government school kids do?)

And then I remembered more. How once Amir

and I became friends the fights stopped. How whenever I was around the other kids would see us playing cricket and watch Amir hit straight sixes and speak Kannada and help decorate our house at Deepavali. But most of all I remembered how when Amir and I were together, they didn't just like him better – they liked me better too. They didn't make fun of me for not having a father or for not always acting like a girl is supposed to act or for being hungry more often than everybody else.

Together, Amir and I kept each other safe.

So who was keeping him safe now?

"What do you mean he doesn't have friends?" I asked.

"He never talks about anyone, and they never come home," Farooq said. "His teachers don't speak to us properly so I'm not sure."

Well that was no surprise. If you remember, no one spoke to me or Amma properly at that school either.

"Plus he hasn't been getting good marks," Farooq said. "Even though he's partly on scholarship, and he has to keep his marks high to keep the money."

That was a surprise. Last year, Amir was my biggest competition for first rank. Usually if I got first, he got second, and if I got second, he got first. I think it's because whenever Amir gets worried or upset, he wants to study. It takes his mind off of everything else. If he isn't doing well, then something is seriously wrong.

"Look, Sarojini, even if he had a million new friends, no one in his life could compare to you," Farooq said.

Hearing Farooq say that felt wonderful and terrible at the same time. In one way, it was exactly what I wanted to hear, because I still wanted to be friends with Amir. But it was also what I didn't want to hear, because it meant that what I had done to Amir was even meaner than I realized.

One of Farooq's friends came and tapped him on the shoulder and told him break was over. After he went back inside, I just stood there for what felt like a long time. Then I walked home. No way could I see Deepti after this. I had too much to think about.

I made a short list of questions, just like really good detectives do when they are choosing their next move. Here they are:

1. Are Amir and I still friends?
2. If we are not still friends, should I try and make us friends again, since I think I'm the one who made us not friends, although I'm not sure?
3. If Amir doesn't like his school, will he come back to our school?
4. If Amir wants to come back to Ambedkar

School, should I keep trying for a seat at Greenhill?

5. If I get a seat at Greenhill, will we both feel better? Or worse?

As you can see, Mrs. Naidu, I am very confused. I have decided that I am going to spend the afternoon thinking about all of this, and then, when I know what I want to do, I'll go meet Deepti.

All the best,
Sarojini

July 21, 2013

Dear Mrs. Naidu,

Remember how I told you yesterday that I was confused? And how today I was going to decide on my next move? And then I'd go see Deepti?

Well I made a decision, Mrs. Naidu. And it's an important one.

I decided that it's time for me to become a fighter.

Just like Amma.

Just like Deepti.

Just like you.

When I went to see Deepti at the construction site, I thought it would be quiet, because it's a Sunday. I was totally wrong. I couldn't tell at first whether she was there or not because it was so busy. There were a bunch of men around this big drill and all I could hear was rat-a-tat-a-tat-a-tat-a-tat. Plus there was dust everywhere, partly from the drill and partly from the women walking up and down with pans of rocks on their heads. I didn't know if any of them were Deepti's parents because I've never met Deepti's Amma, and I had only heard rumours about her Appa – and most of the rumours made me not want to meet him at all.

Finally, I gave up and decided I'd stop by on my way to school tomorrow. Since it was a nice day, I took the long way home, through the pretty, quiet neighbourhood with the houses with lots of bedrooms and flowery gardens. As I was walking, guess what I heard, Mrs. Naidu?

"Oy!"

You know who makes that sound, don't you?

At first I was confused. I looked left and then right. I looked in front of the house and across the street.

Then Deepti said, "Up here!"

You'll never believe where she was, Mrs. Naidu. She was halfway up a tree in front of a mansion that had three floors and at least ten rooms. It even had an iron gate with a sign in English and a brick compound wall. Deepti was balancing on her heels and plucking these tiny, five-petalled white flowers from the tree and putting them in a plastic bag. It looked like she was collecting stars.

"Deepti!" I said – or actually, whispered kind of loudly. "Isn't that stealing?"

Deepti rolled her eyes. "The tree is outside the compound wall. It's not on their property." She didn't whisper.

"I don't think that matters," I said, between my teeth so the neighbours wouldn't hear.

"Fine," she said. "I was done anyway."

She looped the bag over her wrist and came down. From the way she moved, you could tell that she had climbed a million trees before.

"Why do you even need those?" I said.

Deepti shrugged. "Amma says these are powerful for puja."

"Really?" I said. "Maybe I should take some."

"Oh come on," she said, rolling her eyes. "Flowers don't change things. People do."

I thought about that for a second. Well, actually, I said a tiny prayer in my head and asked God not to strike us down.

I thought I was being subtle, but Deepti rolled her eyes again like she knew exactly what was going on inside my brain (and my heart). But instead of saying something else that might bring us bad luck, she said, "Speaking of people, did you meet that lawyer lady?"

"Yes," I said. "That's why I came to find you."

"Then we need to talk. And we can't do it at the construction site. It's too loud."

"I know. Don't you get leave on Sundays?"

Deepti looked at me, hard, and then said, "Sarojini, you have a lot to learn."

I shrugged. "I know a place we can go."

She nodded and fell into step beside me.

('Fell into step beside me' is something else I

learned from detective novels. Actually, from one novel, that was about both crime and romance. When you 'fall into step beside' somebody, you walk next to them, but it's more than that. It's when you go at the same pace and it feels easy and comfortable. Romance is gross, but falling into step beside someone is not.)

As we walked along, I told her about what happened with Vimala Madam. About how the private schools in Bangalore have reservations but are trying to keep kids like me and Deepti out. Then I told her how in Karnataka, we were too old for reservations unless there were extra spots that had not been filled. I was just getting to the part about the other sections when Deepti started complaining.

"Where are you taking me?" she said. We were going through a thick bunch of coconut trees that had lots of bushes and thorns growing between them.

"You're from the village," I said, "you should be used to this."

"I'm not even wearing shoes."

"I thought you were tough."

"I am," Deepti said, shooting me a mean look. "Ow!"

"You can stop fussing now," I said. "We're here."

The special place (which is what Amir and I call it) is this big patch of grass surrounded by coconut trees and flower bushes that's halfway between our homes and the main road. The flowers smell so good that you can't smell the sewage from the hospital or the petrol from the road. Sometimes you can even hear parakeets and mynahs.

"Wow," said Deepti, "it's so... quiet."

I sat on a fallen tree that stretched through the middle of the grass like a park bench in a rich neighbourhood.

"How did you find this place?" she asked, settling down next to me.

"I didn't. Amir did."

"Who's Amir?"

Which just shows you how weird things are, Mrs. Naidu. Nobody ever used to ask me who Amir was because, usually, he was standing right beside me.

"He's my best friend," I said.

"If he's your best friend, how come I've never met him?"

"Because I'm not sure if we're friends anymore." It was the first time I had said it out loud. It felt scary, but then, considering how much scary stuff I've been doing lately, it was really just one more thing. "He goes to another school now. Actually, he goes to Greenhill."

Deepti turned and looked off into the distance, and said, quietly, "So that's why you asked for a seat."

I nodded. "I thought he liked it there. But now I'm not so sure."

"Of course he doesn't like it," Deepti said, narrowing her eyes at me.

(I'm starting to understand Deepti's looks. This one meant, 'For a city girl, you sure can be slow.')

(She gives me that one a lot.)

"What do you mean?" I asked.

"His life may be different," she said. "But *he's* not different. Those rich kids, they can always tell who the poor kids are. We're the ones who build their houses and sweep their floors. They're used to ordering us around or ignoring us, not being in class with us."

It's not like I didn't notice this before, Mrs. Naidu. It's hard *not* to notice the invisible wall between kids like me and kids who go to Greenhill. I see the kids from the houses where Amma works getting on those bright yellow school vans pretty much every day, when I'm walking to school. I know they see me too, but we never wave.

"Who cares about the students," I said. "At least he has better teachers than us."

"Are you kidding? The adults are worse than the kids. When I went to St. Augustina they wouldn't even let me put my brother down on the floor. Like some four-year-old kid is going to tear the place apart?"

"It was the same at Greenhill. The secretary put this weird cleaning stuff on her hand after Amma touched her. It smelled like a hospital or something."

"Not that we're any better," Deepti said. "I'm sure plenty of people told you not to be friends with me because we live at the construction site."

I thought about Hema Aunty. "Not plenty of people. But some."

"See?" Deepti said. "Annie Miss isn't like that though. She cares about all of us. That's why she's always saying all that stuff about believing in us. And same with Abhi's anganwadi teacher – I saw her buy eggs for the kids when the rations didn't come."

"Our old headmistress was like that too. Once she saw my fancy dress was too tight and she bought me a new one. She told me it used to be her daughter's, but the price tags were still on it."

"No one at Greenhill would do that."

"They might."

Deepti shrugged, but I could tell she didn't think so.

"Besides," she said. "I like the kids at our school. I don't see why we have to go somewhere else."

That's when I had a breakthrough.

(In case you don't know, Mrs. Naidu, detectives get a 'breakthrough' before they solve cases. A breakthrough is when all the clues come together and the detectives figure out who did it, and the best way to catch the criminal. Deepti and I aren't catching criminals here, but we *are* working on a case: the case of how to fix ~~my life~~ our lives.)

Here is what I figured out in my breakthrough:

1.   How to get Amir to be my friend again.

2.   How to get Amir and Deepti to be friends, so all three of us can be together.

3.   How to make sure we all go to a good school so that when we grow up we can live in the same neighbourhood, which will be a nice neighbourhood with roofs and water and people who don't think we're dirty or diseased.

"Deepti," I said. "I need to tell you about the rest of RTE."

Do you remember what is in the rest of RTE, Mrs. Naidu?

In a good detective story, the detective doesn't reveal the answer to the questions right away. Annie Miss told me that in English, it's called 'leaving the reader in suspense.' So I'm going to leave you in suspense.

(I hope you don't mind, Mrs. Naidu.)

All the best,
Sarojini

July 22, 2013

Dear Mrs. Naidu,

Well, Mrs. Naidu? Did you review the evidence? Did you draw any conclusions?

I think you probably did, since you are a genius (but not an evil one). Just in case you didn't, I'll tell you what happened at Child Rights Club today.

Remember how at the beginning of the last meeting there were five of us? This time there were just two: me and Deepti. When she saw us, Annie Miss sighed and said, "I wish the rest of your class cared as much about rights as you two."

Deepti made a kind of snorting noise, which I think was the sound of her pushing a mean laugh back down inside of herself. I tried to drown it out before Miss could feel bad.

"Actually, we wanted to talk to you about them," I said. "Our rights, I mean. If that's okay."

Deepti rolled her eyes but Miss said, "Of course, Sarojini. You can talk to me about anything."

(Why do adults always say that?)

Deepti made that noise again, except this time she pretended to cough, but that didn't work because she sounded like she was dying of some weird sarcastic laughing disease, so I said really loudly. "We want to talk about RTE."

"No need to shout, Sarojini," Miss said.

I stopped shouting and Deepti stopped laughing-snorting-coughing-dying-eye-rolling and we told her our idea. And when I say 'we', I really mean that.

We sounded like this:

"I went to see this lawyer, and she told me that RTE is more than just section twelve –"

"Section twelve is reservations. But there's this whole other part about government schools–"

"It says they're supposed to have playgrounds and drinking water –"

"But also, teachers aren't supposed to hit us. It's called corporal punishment and it's not allowed –"

"And we're supposed to have classes for out-of-school kids who are behind –"

"Stop," Miss said. She was smiling, and her eyes were kind of shiny. "One at a time."

Deepti stopped talking so I could tell Miss about going to see Vimala Madam. Then I stopped talking so Deepti could tell Miss about how we decided that we like our government school (or, actually, the people at our government school) better than any private school (or, actually, the people at *certain* private schools). So instead of using the law to get seats somewhere else, we wanted to use the law to fix Ambedkar Government School.

"What do you mean by 'fix'?" Miss asked.

That started us off again, tripping over each other's words.

"Repair the hole in the gate – "

"Build a playground – "

"Redo the compound wall – "

"Slow down, slow down," Miss said. "Let's make a list."

Here is the list we wrote after we slowed down:

1. Repair hole in gate
2. Clean up and paint compound wall
3. Build a playground
4. Get drinking water
5. Hire someone to help kids like Deepti who haven't been in school for a while
6. Get training for teachers on discipline (Miss added this – she says it's so teachers will stop hitting us).

When we were done, Miss's eyes were even shinier. She put down her pencil and took our hands and then kind of stared out into space. I looked at Deepti and Deepti did her special eye-roll that means, "Ugh, another just-and-beautiful-world moment."

"Girls," Miss said, in a voice that was low and scratchy, "I believe in you. And I believe in us. I believe that together, we can do this. But it's not going to be easy. There will be many obstacles in our way and many people who will discourage us."

Then Miss put our hands in the middle of the table and folded her hands over them and stared at us with these wide, serious eyes like an actress in a Kannada serial who is totally overdoing it.

"Are you ready to struggle?" she said.

At first we didn't realize that she wanted an answer. But when we didn't say anything, she kept that whole daughter-in-law-in-a-serial thing going, so we both spoke.

"I guess so," I said.

"Sure," said Deepti.

"Even if we don't succeed, think of how much we will learn together," Miss said, sighing and looking out the window. She kept gripping our hands, and I really felt like I was on TV.

"Students like you are the reason I became a teacher," Miss said eventually, and her voice was all squishy and wobbly and full of water.

"Thank you, Miss," Deepti said. She didn't roll her eyes, but I know she wanted to.

(To be completely honest, Mrs. Naidu, so did I.)

"What's our next move?" I asked, partly because I wanted to know, and partly because it's how detectives talk.

We decided that I'd go back to Vimala Madam so we can start getting all the items on our list. (Or "so we can begin our struggle," as Miss said.)

It's not exactly pushing the Britishers out of India, or getting women the right to vote. But it's still my first fight, Mrs. Naidu, and my first time being a fighter. I hope I do alright.

All the best,
Sarojini

Dear Mrs. Naidu,

After the Child Rights Club meeting, I was excited.

I was excited about the plan I made with Deepti and Miss.

But I was also excited about the secret plan I made with myself.

(In case you couldn't figure out my secret plan – which I think you did, seeing as you are one of the smartest ~~women~~ people ever in history – I'll take away the suspense. The secret plan is to make Ambedkar School so great that Amir will want to come back. Then, Amir will meet Deepti, and all three of us will be best friends together. This is even better than my original plan, because I will have two best friends at my school instead of just one.)

You know what I was not excited about?

Seeing Vimala Madam again.

I know, I know. Last time things went pretty well.

(Okay, maybe not pretty well. Maybe more like, not so bad.)

But do you think Vimala Madam stapled her eyebrow in place?

Do you think she got out a big bottle of Fevicol and attached her glasses to her nose?

Do you think she's combed her hair?

No, neither do I.

Since just going past the front door of the building makes my stomach twist, I wasn't sure when I would ever feel brave enough to see Madam at her flat again. So this time, I didn't tell Amma I was coming. I just showed up.

She was surprised when she opened the door.

"Sarojini," Amma said – actually she kind of hissed, like a snake, or maybe a really angry cat. "What are you doing here?"

"I'm coming from school," I said. Then I thought for a second, and asked, hopefully, "Am I allowed to go home by myself now?"

"Of course not," Amma said – or actually, spat. (Definitely an angry cat.)

"I'm just following the rules," I said. "Plus Madam said that I had to tell her what happened with my, um, school project. Is she home?"

"She's in her study," Amma said. "When she's in there she doesn't like to be disturbed."

"But wouldn't it be disrespectful if I didn't tell her what happened?" I asked. And then, just in case, I added, "I mean, it *is* a school project and everything."

If there's one thing Amma can't stand, it's

disrespect. And as you know, Mrs. Naidu, she never says no to anything that has to do with school.

Well, hardly ever.

Amma folded her arms across her chest and said, "Madam is very busy. You can't just expect her to be free when it's convenient for you."

(If I do become a lawyer – which I'm not saying I will – I don't think any case will ever be as hard as the case of getting Amma to let me do what I want.)

"But Amma –"

"Sit quietly and do your schoolwork," Amma said. "Don't say anything or eat anything or touch anything."

"Amma, can't I just – "

"What did I just say?" Amma said. "Don't. Say. Anything."

(Can you believe I was disappointed about *not* seeing Vimala Madam?)

I sighed and sat down and started doing my maths homework – which, by the way, was extremely frustrating because Amma kept looking over my shoulder and correcting me before I even finished any of the problems, because even though she never completed Class Five she is better at maths than me or Amir or Deepti or probably even our maths teacher – when I heard a door bang across the house.

A heavy door.

A heavy, wooden door.

"Sujatha, would you make me some tea?" Vimala Madam asked as she walked through the heavy door and between her heavy furniture and past her heavy books to her kitchen that, thanks to Amma, smelled delicious.

Where she saw me.

Madam pulled her glasses down her nose.

She pushed her one eyebrow up her forehead.

She ran her hand through her hair.

Then, she sat down on the flimsy plastic chair next to the flimsy plastic table where I was doing my maths and she asked, "Sarojini. Do you, by any chance, enjoy tea?"

She spoke to me like I was a lawyer and not a Class Six student.

"Um," I said.

"Sarojini won't have any, Madam," Amma said. "But I'll make some for you."

Vimala Madam nodded and leaned across the table, clasping her hands in front of her, and running her hand through her hair one more time (I guess just to make sure it was messy enough). "Now then, Sarojini," she said. "I believe I am owed an update."

"Yes, Madam," I said.

Mrs. Naidu, I read that when you made speeches

all over the world, people liked you so much that they wrote about you in newspapers and elected you to lots of important positions, like the president of the South African Indian Congress and the president of the East African Indian Congress. I read that your speeches in England and America and Kenya and South Africa were about how women should be allowed to vote and girls should get an education and how all countries that the Britishers had taken over should be set free.

It seems like when you made those speeches, people listened.

Because everything that you said should happen *did* happen, which means, after a long time, people actually did what you told them to do.

But do you remember being a kid, Mrs. Naidu?

Do you remember how nobody wanted to listen to you because they thought you should listen to them instead?

Do you remember how they were more interested in telling you what to do than hearing about what *you* wanted to do?

Well, Vimala Madam didn't treat me like a kid. She treated me like she would've treated you – like I was someone who had something important to say. She didn't interrupt me once. Not when I told her about how Deepti and I had talked about getting seats in a private school, but then realized that we didn't want to be away from our teachers and our friends who care about us. Not when I talked about how Deepti and I thought that maybe if we fixed our school, more people would come, and our brains and hearts could grow more. Not when I showed her the list we made in Child Rights Club, and told her how Annie Miss said that she'd help us, but what we really needed was help from someone who knew about laws.

By the time I stopped, Vimala Madam was leaning back in her chair, her arms crossed, her spectacles on top of her head. She nodded slowly, looking down her pointy nose at me, like she was deciding whether to use her evil genius to help me or to end the world.

I sat on my hands so she wouldn't see they were shaking.

"My dear, I am so pleased," she said.

(Honestly, Mrs. Naidu, if that's what she looks like when she's pleased, I never want to see her unpleased.)

"When the founders of this country wrote the Constitution, they envisioned an India in which every child had access to an excellent education," she went on.

"Founders like Sarojini Naidu, Madam?"

"Especially Sarojini Naidu," she said. "I see you are reading the book I gave you. If so, you know that your namesake was particularly motivated to make sure that girls could be educated."

(I nodded, but actually, Mrs. Naidu, I have no idea what a namesake is – except that now I know that you are mine.)

"Unfortunately, their vision was never properly realized. This is why laws like the Right to Free and Compulsory Education Act of 2009 are necessary even today. Speaking of which," she said, "do you have that circular with you? Perhaps we can find some clues that will help us decide our next move."

(Did you catch that, Mrs. Naidu? Clues? Our next move?)

(I guess maybe lawyers are sort of like detectives.)

Vimala Madam and I sat with the pamphlet and looked for clues so we could decide our next move. She turned to the very end – which she showed me was called 'The Schedule,' even though it's a list of stuff, not a list of timings, which is what I thought a schedule was – and showed me how a lot of what we wanted, like drinking water and a playground, are mandatory, which means the government has to give them to us. (I sort of knew that already, Mrs. Naidu, since she showed me last time too.) Then she showed me the part of the law that says how each school has to have a management committee (she said in Karnataka we call it an SDMC which stands for School Development Management Committee). She said the SDMC comes up with a school development plan, which is kind of like a list of things to ask for to make our school better – in fact, it's a lot like the list we'd already made.

"Remember, we discussed that the SDMC should include parents, teachers, local officials, and students," Vimala Madam said. "It should have nine people. Three-quarters of the committee should be parents and at least half should be women."

It sounded like a math problem, Mrs. Naidu, which was why I suddenly remembered that Amma was in the kitchen. I think Madam remembered too, because we both looked up at the same time.

Amma was scrubbing the sink really hard.

"Sujatha," Madam said to Amma. "You should join this committee. You'd be a strong leader, and you'd set an excellent example for Sarojini."

Amma stopped scrubbing and smiled at Madam. It wasn't a typical Amma smile though – usually, her smiles go straight through her, and they fill up her whole body with light. This smile was just on the surface. There wasn't light underneath, exactly, but there may have been another kind of glow – a little like fire.

"Yes, Madam," Amma said. Which you'll notice, is not exactly a response to Vimala Madam's suggestion.

That's when I knew I was in trouble, even though I wasn't sure why.

Madam, though, had no idea.

"Well then," Madam said. "Sarojini, darling, you have the same assignment as last time. Please come back and tell me what you decide. But no matter what, remember," she said, holding up the pamphlet and kind of rattling it with one hand. With the other she (you guessed it) put her glasses down her nose so she could peer over them at me. "The law is on your side. And the law is a powerful thing."

It was really like an evil genius move, Mrs. Naidu, except what Madam was saying was the opposite of evil. It was confusing, but at least I knew now she wasn't going to end the world.

"Yes Madam," I said, putting the law and my maths homework in my bag and standing up. I glanced over at Amma, and my legs started shaking.

"We should go," Amma said then. She dug her fingers into my wrist so hard that I had to stop myself from gasping. (Which, by the way, I think is corporal punishment.) "It's getting late, and Sarojini still has a lot of homework to finish."

"Of course, of course," Madam said. "School comes first. I very much enjoy our conversations, Sarojini. Do come by as often as you can."

"Yes, Madam," I said between my teeth. Amma's

death grip was making my wrist throb and my heart race.

Amma kind of jerked us both outside. Vimala Madam kept the door open and waved as we walked down the huge driveway. The second we were out of sight, Amma dropped my wrist and leaned very close to me, shooting all kinds of laser beams out of her eyes.

"You told me you were getting help on a school assignment," she said – or, more accurately, she barked.

(I hope Vimala Madam isn't contagious, Mrs. Naidu.)

"It was for Child Rights Club," I said. "Which is at school."

"A club is not a class," Amma said. "What do you think you're doing, starting all this nonsense?"

"But our club wants to improve our school," I said. "I thought you'd be proud. You always say education is the most important thing. Why are you so angry?"

"That's *exactly* why I'm angry," Amma said. "You're supposed to be studying, not worrying about drinking water and toilets and god knows what else you and that construction site girl have been carrying on about."

"Deepti," I whispered. "Her name is Deepti."

Amma ignored me, and said, "My job is to make

sure you go to a good school. Your job is to get good marks. It is *not* to create problems."

"I'm trying to fix problems," I said, "not create them."

"You're twelve years old. You should not be fixing anything." She turned and started walking quickly down the main road. I had to scramble to keep up with her.

"Amma, I can't stop now. I promised Deepti," I panted.

"Deepti and that family of hers will be gone in a month. She'll be away from all the galatta and where will you be? Stuck here."

"But you heard Madam. She says I'm making the right decision. And she says she does cases like this all the time, she told me– "

"That's another thing," Amma said. "I need this job. If you keep interacting with Madam this way, asking her for help, dragging her into our problems, she'll get tired of us and I'll lose my best-paying house."

"But you just took on so many new houses!"

"Of course I did. How else are we going to pay for your supposedly free seat?"

"What are you talking about?" Amma and I never talked about Greenhill after that day, and I thought the whole thing was over. But even if it wasn't over, and Amma was trying to get me in, why would she need money for a free seat? That's the whole point – when something is free, you don't *need* money for it.

Amma stopped walking. She turned around, leaned over, and put her hands on my shoulders, the way she used to when I was little and she had to tell me something difficult, like that Appa had left or we didn't have enough food for dinner.

"You don't know what happened, do you?"

First, I shook my head.

But then I remembered the clues:

1. How the hard glittery woman at Greenhill passed Amma a piece of paper.
2. How Amma said that thing about honesty.
3. How Hema Aunty and Nimisha Aunty complained about the price of free seats.

"They want you to pay a bribe," I said, slowly, as I was drawing my conclusion. "You've got all these extra houses so you can pay for my seat."

Amma didn't say anything at first. But then, after a minute, she whispered, "You know I'll do anything for your future, ma. But if you stir up trouble, you'll get a reputation, and no one will take you no matter how much we pay."

It felt like all the traffic on the main road got louder and faster and the air got thicker and dustier and more confusing.

But maybe it wasn't the main road. Maybe it was the inside of my head.

"Amma, I don't want to go to a posh school. Especially one that is corrupt. If I go there, what will happen to my heart? It definitely won't grow like Annie Miss thinks it should."

"Darling, I know you think you can change Ambedkar School. But no matter how many changes you make, it won't help. Government school students don't have a future. Look at me – I went to a government school. I even won prizes and topped my exams. But what do I do now? I wash dishes and sweep floors."

Amma stopped being angry, then – or at least, she stopped being angry at me. She kept being angry at the world. "For you, it will be different."

We walked the rest of the way home in silence. I don't know what Amma was thinking about – maybe about my future at Greenhill or how she was going to raise the money for the bribe.

But I was thinking about what she said.

I thought about how all the kids I knew in our neighbourhood had parents who went to government schools.

I thought about how so many of us wore old clothes or were always hungry or had to leave school to work, even though our parents already worked all day, and sometimes all night.

I thought about how none of the detectives I read about could have gone to government schools.

Most of all, I thought about how I always imagined that if I ever became fighter, Amma would be on my side.

Right now, my thoughts feel more tangled up than Bangalore traffic, and I don't know what side I'm on.

But I have a feeling it's not Amma's.

All the best,
Sarojini

July 27, 2013

Dear Mrs. Naidu,

It's Saturday, Mrs. Naidu, so we only had a half day of school. I spent the afternoon reading about you. I just finished the part where you became friends with an American woman named Jane Addams. She came all the way to India to support you when you were elected to the municipal government in Mumbai (which used to be called Bombay ~~when you were alive before you died~~ when you lived there), and you went all the way to visit her in the United States, to a city called Chicago. You were probably friends because you had a lot in common: she cared about women's rights and education, and she was smart and famous and wrote a ton of books. Just like you.

But you know what else this book says? It says that the American government thought that Mrs. Addams was one of the most dangerous women in the world. That means that you could've gotten in a lot of trouble for being friends with her, Mrs. Naidu.

Then I started thinking – the Britishers probably called you dangerous too. So that means that Mrs.

Addams could have gotten in trouble for being friends with you.

Mrs. Naidu, how did you know that you should be friends with Mrs. Addams even though people said she was dangerous?

I was wondering about it this morning, when Deepti was waiting at the construction site with Abhi so the three of us could walk to school together, like we do every day now.

When I said hi to Deepti, she rolled her eyes. Then she pointed to Abhi who, as usual, was singing.

Abhi used to be quiet when we went to school, but ever since he started at the anganwadi, he's always got some rhyme that he repeats over and over and over again. Today he was singing something about alphabets and freedom fighters.

"ABCDEFG, G is the name of Gandhiji," he said.

"Hi Abhi," I said.

"HIJKLMNOP, P is the name of Panditji," he replied.

(I told him to add you when he got to S, Mrs. Naidu, but he wouldn't do it. I'll keep trying.)

"How long has he been like this?" I asked Deepti.

"Since Wednesday. First he only knew up to G. Now he knows the whole thing."

"Wow. And he hasn't stopped?"

"Nope. But at least he knows his ABCs – pretty

good since he's only four years old, you know, and nobody in our family speaks English." Deepti shrugged and rolled her eyes again, but she was sort of smiling, like she was proud but trying to hide it. "Did you go see the evil genius?"

I said yes, and I told Deepti ~~the whole story~~ the part of the story where Vimala Madam said we need to form a committee and then get them to approve all our ideas.

"Who's on the committee again?" she asked.

"Teachers, parents, and students. But there has to be nine people, and three fourths of them have to be parents. Oh, and half of them have to be women."

"Students are no problem. We're students."

"Me too," Abhi said.

"Not you," Deepti said. Abhi looked like he was about to cry, so Deepti chanted, "Q-R-S-T-U-V?"

"V is the name of Vajpaiji!" Abhi sang.

"Annie Miss can be the teacher," I said. "And we're all women – or, girls and women, I guess. But anyway that's good."

"So all we need are parents," Deepti said. "Your Amma will do it."

"Um, well – she's actually pretty busy right now," I said, swallowing hard. "I mean, she's just started a bunch of new houses and stuff."

I thought Deepti would roll her eyes or spit or

something. But instead, she put her arm around my shoulder.

"I can't imagine if my Appa wasn't around."

I probably shouldn't have done this, Mrs. Naidu, but I blurted out, "Your Appa? Isn't he useless?"

"He drinks a lot," Deepti admitted, "but at least he gives us money every month. Not as much as he should, but it's something. And at least Amma and Abhi and I aren't afraid that someone is going to come take advantage of us because there's no man around."

Imagine that, Mrs. Naidu. Here I was feeling sorry for Deepti, and this whole time, she was feeling sorry for me!

"It's not so bad. At least we stay in one place."

Deepti shrugged and said, "Yeah, well. We're lucky we both have families who are speaking to us and care about us in their own odd ways."

I thought of Amma then. "Do you think we're going to get in trouble for doing this?"

"Probably."

"Wait, really?"

"Really."

"You're not worried?"

"I'm worried about a lot more than getting in trouble," Deepti said. "I'm worried that my Amma and Appa will never make enough money to keep our farm, which is the whole reason we came to work in Bangalore in the first place. I'm worried Appa is going to get so drunk one night that he won't come home. I'm worried Amma isn't going to find the next job for us and that we'll have nowhere to live and nothing to eat. I'm worried that my parents or Abhi are going to get hurt or maybe even die at the site. It happens a lot, you know."

"I didn't know you worried about all that," I said, looking at Deepti out of the corner of my eye. Usually she acted so light and careless. Now, it was like all the years of her life were pressing down on her skinny shoulders – and even though her whole life is technically only twelve years, her problems made it sound more like a hundred.

"I try not to talk about it – or, actually, think about it – because if I let worrying stop me, I'd never do anything. I'd never try to change anything. And if I don't change things, then nobody else is going to, and the worries will just go on forever – for Amma and Appa, and for me and Abhi, and probably for my kids, and even my kids' kids. It'll never end. And that's my biggest worry of all."

For a while, we let Deepti's words twist in the damp morning wind. I thought about how Amma must have felt when Appa left us alone in a strange city when I wasn't even able to talk yet. Back then, Amma wasn't much older than me and Deepti are now. Her worries were probably a lot like Deepti's. Which, actually, are a lot like mine.

Suddenly Abhi started jumping up and down and saying, "School school school school school!"

"Calm down," Deepti said, scooping him up. But he kept bouncing on her hip and started chanting some rhyme about a monkey drinking bisi bisi payasa before going to anganwadi.

He launched himself off of Deepti's hip and took off across the compound, the bottoms of his bare feet flashing browner and browner as they caked with muddy earth.

"He does this every time he sees the gate," Deepti said.

"Imagine how he'll feel when we fix it," I said.

"Yeah," Deepti said, smiling. "Just imagine."

All the best,
Sarojini

August 1, 2013

Dear Mrs. Naidu,

Today was a big day, Mrs. Naidu, because we officially started the plan to fix our school. I thought once we started I'd be happy and proud. But I'm not, really. I'm… well… I'm not sure how I feel, which I guess is why I'm writing you this letter.

Our plan has four steps. Step One is forming the SDMC. Step Two is making a school development plan, Step Three is getting money from the government to pay for what we need, and Step Four is doing all the stuff on our list so we can fix our school. Today we didn't really do step one, but we did something we had to do before Step One. So I guess what we did was actually Step 0, or maybe Step ½.

(I think you'll agree, Mrs. Naidu, whether it's four steps or four-and-a-half steps, it's a pretty fast plan. Much faster than your plan to make the British quit India, which probably had at least a hundred steps, or maybe even a thousand. Definitely more than four-and-a-half.)

Anyway Step 0, or ½, or whatever you want to call it, was asking the Headmaster if it was okay for us to form the committee. We went to see him this morning because we had no choice: the HM only comes in on the first of the month. No one knows where he goes the rest of the time, because no one knows where he lives. Everyone says he has another job, but I can't picture him going to office or driving an auto or doing anything, really, besides grumbling.

I've always thought our HM looks kind of like a criminal sidekick in a Kannada movie. He's got a big, thick moustache that curls a little at the ends and bushy black hair that sticks straight up from his head. He's also kind of square and solid looking, like if he got angry he could pick up a whole box of books and throw them across the room. Except that he wouldn't get angry unless someone told him to, because he's not the kind of person who does things on his own. That's why he's the criminal sidekick, not the evil genius – he's like a bodyguard, or the guy who drives the getaway car who's listed as 'Kalla #3' in the credits.

(I guess it's funny that I don't think he'd be the person running things, considering that he runs our school.)

Mrs. Naidu, I know from this book I'm reading that your sister was an HM at a school she started in Lahore, which used to be India, but is now Pakistan. So you know what an HM is supposed to be like, and you also know what happens to a school when the HM doesn't do his (or her) job.

So before you think badly of us, Mrs. Naidu, I should tell you that it wasn't always like this at Ambedkar School. Our old HM, Janaki Madam, was like your sister: she was there every day for years and years and years – in fact, she had been the HM for a lot of my classmates' parents. She came to school every day. She arrived early, she stayed late, and she knew everything about everyone. If kids were absent a lot, she'd go to their houses and talk to their families. When you saw Janaki Madam go to someone's house, you knew things were going to get better. After her visits, Appas and Ammas got jobs, rents got paid, food started showing up regularly – sometimes, all of those things happened at once.

Everyone loved Janaki Madam, but she completed 35 years of service and decided to retire. She still lives around here, and I sometimes see her when I buy the greens Amma likes at the carts near Janaki Madam's house. I miss seeing her at school, though, and I especially miss stopping by her office after class – she used to keep English and Kannada picture books on her desk so we could practice reading in both languages while she filled out registers and made lots of phone calls. Sometimes I was worried that we were disturbing her, but she told me that she liked having us around. She said it gave her energy.

This new HM though? He's not like that. It's not that he likes having us around or that he dislikes it – it's that he doesn't notice us at all.

It felt strange to be back in the office for the first time in three years. Some things were the same – like Janaki Madam's metal desk, which was kind of slanted and had a crooked drawer that you could tell would never close no matter how much you forced it. But a lot of things were different, like the stacks and stacks of registers and papers sitting on the desk collecting dust and waiting for signatures (Janaki Madam always did her work right away and then put everything in files, and she dusted every day), and the blank walls (Janaki Madam used to cover them with our artwork and tests where we scored 100%), and the stack of cardboard boxes full of new uniforms (Janaki Madam used to pass them out the first week, or even before if you stopped by and asked her).

When we walked in, the HM was writing in a register. Without looking up, he asked "Who are you?"

Well, that was a bad start. Especially if you're talking to Deepti.

"We're students here," Deepti said. "Don't you even recognize your own students?"

"Sir," Miss said, putting her arms around our shoulders like she wanted to protect me from the

HM, and the HM from Deepti, "Sarojini and Deepti are two of my brightest students."

Great, I thought. Now he knows our names.

"Sir," I said, "we want your permission to start a committee to improve the school."

He didn't react, but I kept going, trying to remember the lines that Miss and Deepti had made me rehearse yesterday afternoon.

"We want to make some simple changes that will improve our education and will reflect positively on our community," I said.

"Basically, this whole thing will make you look good," Deepti said, which probably was true, but definitely was not something we agreed to say. "We'll do all the work and you'll get all the credit."

I elbowed her, and she said, "Ow!" and then rubbed her arm and said, "What?"

The HM didn't say anything. He just kept writing.

Deepti took a breath like she was about to speak again, and I think Miss noticed, because she quickly said, "Sir?"

The HM put his pencil down and folded his hands on the register.

"I was at my last school for seventeen years before they transferred me here," he said, staring at the register instead of us. "I loved that school. I started it with my wife. We bought all the books, hired all the teachers – we even put our own money into the building costs when the government funds didn't come on time. We sent our children there, even though we could've put them in private school. We wanted to set an example. Of course, at the time, it felt like we had hundreds of children – our students were our family."

"So why'd you leave?" Deepti asked. She didn't say it very politely, but the HM didn't seem to notice.

"The government closed it," he said. "Our enrollment was too low. I did everything I could to save it. I started all kinds of committees. Committees for new toilets and new textbooks and new teacher recruitment. You know what came out of those committees? Nothing. No toilets. No textbooks. No teachers."

The HM told us all this like he was reciting an exam. His voice was flat, and if you didn't listen to the words, you wouldn't know that the story was sad.

"Committees," he said, "are useless."

I should've been angry, Mrs. Naidu. Thanks to the HM, it seemed like we weren't even going to get through Step ½, let alone Step One. But honestly, I didn't blame him. I know enough grown ups to know that there's nothing harder than watching your dreams fall apart, especially when you put your whole life into them. Sometimes those dreams are schools. Sometimes they're farms, or children, or marriages.

"I don't know what I'd do if Ambedkar School closed," I thought. But then, too late, I realized that I didn't think it – I said it out loud.

The HM looked surprised too, like he had forgotten I was there. After a minute, he picked up his pencil and started writing again. Miss silently motioned that we should leave.

We were nearly out the door when the HM said, "Do whatever you want. Just don't ask for money, because we have none. And don't ask me questions, because I don't want to know about any of it."

"Thank you sir," Miss said.

"You're just wasting your time," the HM said.

And that was that.

Like I said, Mrs. Naidu, I should have been happy because now we can get to Step One. Deepti and Miss were certainly were – when we left the office, Deepti started doing a victory dance and Miss's eyes got all just-and-beautiful-world-y.

"I'm so proud of you," she said.

"Yeah!" Deepti whooped. "Dance with me!" She took my hand and started twirling in circles.

"See you girls tomorrow," Miss said, as Deepti pulled me towards the anganwadi to pick up Abhi.

I guess I wasn't shaking my hips hard enough,

because Deepti, still dancing, said, "What's the matter?"

"I don't know," I said. "It's the HM."

"What about him?"

"I've spent all this time thinking he was useless, and it turns out that he was like Janaki Madam. But look at him now. He's lost everything – his school, his students, hope. Everything."

"But he has new students and a new school," Deepti said. "He has a second chance and he doesn't want to take it. He didn't *lose* hope. He gave it up."

"I guess you're right."

But I'm not sure, Mrs. Naidu. When you think about all the things that could go wrong in our plan, even though it's only four steps (or maybe four and a half, depending on how you look at it), it makes me wonder how I'll feel if we try and try and try and it doesn't work.

Will we turn out like HM Sir and not care about anything and be sad all the time?

Did you ever ~~lose~~ give up hope, Mrs. Naidu?

Will I?

All the best,
Sarojini

August 3, 2013

Dear Mrs. Naidu,

Mrs. Naidu, I guess I still have a lot to learn about fighting.

After we met with the HM and finished Step ½, our next move was Step One, which is convening the SDMC.

('Convening' is an English word that means bringing people together. It's not a detective word – it's a lawyer word. It might also be a politician word, but I'm not sure.)

Out of all four steps, I thought convening would be the easiest. Vimala Madam said the SDMC should have nine people. Me, Deepti, and Annie Mam are three. So we only needed six more, and they all had to be parents, mostly mothers so that we could make sure that the committee was 50% women.

(Who knew that convening took so much math? I wonder if lawyering does too.)

You know who Deepti and I know a lot of? Mothers. If you remember, Mrs. Naidu, in my neighbourhood I know everyone and everyone knows me. As for Deepti, once she and Abhi registered at Ambedkar School, she took a bunch of the other kids from the construction site and got them enrolled too, so all the Ammas love her, and will pretty much do anything she tells them to do.

Between the two of us, how hard could it be?

The answer is: very, very, *very* hard.

Here is the list of people I asked, and what they said:

1. Kamala Aunty won't leave the area without her husband, but her husband won't come to the meeting because school is women's business.
2. Mary Aunty is going to enroll Joseph in private school so she doesn't want to waste her time.
3. Amina Aunty says she doesn't want to be involved in anything that the HM is involved in. She says she met him once, and it was one time too many.
4. Nimisha Aunty doesn't want to leave the house she works in and lose pay for some useless meeting that won't get us anywhere anyway.
5. Hema Aunty says she is not in the mood to watch people break promises because she gets enough of that from her husband, not to mention the local leader who *still* hasn't gotten us new roofs.

I didn't mean to, Mrs. Naidu, but just by asking about the SDMC, I started an aunty galatta, which everyone knows is the worst kind of galatta because it is the loudest and the hardest to stop. By the time I spoke to Hema Aunty, there was a whole crowd of aunties telling me all the reasons why they weren't coming and why I should just give up. All of them were talking at me but also at each other, and their words kept slamming against the place in my heart that was supposed to be growing.

"You're going to form a committee that's only women and children?" Hema Aunty said. "Who listens to women and children?"

"Definitely not that HM," Amina Aunty said. "That man doesn't listen and he doesn't do anything."

"But Aunty," I said (although I wasn't sure which aunty I meant), "we spoke to a lawyer who is going to help us, and she says–"

"That woman your mother works for?" Nimisha Aunty said – actually, she kind of spat. "Those rich people love to help us for a second and feel good. Then when things fall apart, they're nowhere to be found."

"None of you should be bothering with that school to begin with," Mary Aunty said. "If the government runs it, it won't work."

"That's the point," I said. "The government is *supposed* to make the schools work. It's in the Constitution."

"Constitution?" Amina Aunty laughed. "Where

are you learning these big English words? The Constitution is not for people like us. It's for people like your lawyer friend."

"But it *is* for us!" I said, thinking of you, Mrs. Naidu. "Besides, the government schools may not work now, but they're the schools we have. I don't know anyone who has gotten into a private school reservation seat. Do you?"

"Sarojini, darling, you're such a sweet girl," Kamala Aunty said in her gentle, Kamala Aunty way. "You get such good marks and are so helpful to your mother. Just leave things be."

When I came home, I was so angry, I couldn't concentrate on my assignment, so I picked up the book about you. I read about how during the freedom movement, when you became the leader of the agitation in Dharasana, you convinced all the protestors to stay together and remain calm, even when the Britishers beat Indians with lathis. All our teachers say Dharasana was the protest that made people around the world realize that the British were being unfair to Indians, and that they should leave.

(It's funny, Mrs. Naidu, because even though our teachers made us memorize all of these things about Dharasana, they never told us that you were the one who led it.)

I looked at the photos of Dharasana in the book, and it seems like there were lots of aunties there.

In fact, if I squint my eyes and turn the page to a certain angle, the aunties look like Nimisha Aunty and Kamala Aunty and Amina Aunty and Mary Aunty and Hema Aunty and even Amma.

Especially Amma.

What did you say to them at Dharasana, Mrs. Naidu?

How did you make them fight alongside you, even if you didn't know if you would succeed?

I'm looking for the right words, Mrs. Naidu. But I can't seem to find them anywhere.

All the best,
Sarojini

August 5, 2013

Dear Mrs. Naidu,

It turns out that Deepti didn't do much better at getting people to join the SDMC. She and I were supposed to meet before class, but Abhi is going through this phase where he won't get dressed in the mornings because he wants a school uniform like the Class One kids, so Deepti came in late after struggling with him, and when she saw me she shrugged and rolled her tired black eyes.

(Which, as you know, Mrs. Naidu, is the main thing Deepti does with her eyes.)

We didn't get to really talk until we were walking home and Deepti said, "Amma's coming. Everybody else said they weren't sure, which I think means no. How many people did you get?"

"None," I said.

I guess Deepti thought she heard me wrong, because right then Abhi ran up to us and started a new rhyme – something in Kannada about a crow – because she scooped him up and said, "In your whole neighbourhood, you only got one?"

"Down!" Abhi said.

"I got *none*," I repeated. "Zero. Nobody."

"Up!" Abhi said, as soon as his feet touched the ground.

"What?" Deepti said, carrying him again. "Why?"

"They can't leave work," I said. "They don't want to come without their husbands. They think the HM is useless. They think the school is useless, we're useless, and this whole idea is useless."

"Down!" Abhi said, wiggling.

Deepti put him on the ground and said, "You told them how we have a famous lawyer and the thing about the Constitution and how the reservations are nonsense?"

(Only she didn't say "nonsense," Mrs. Naidu. She said something much worse.)

"I told them," I said.

Deepti groaned and said, "Idiots."

(Only she didn't say "idiots.")

"Up!" Abhi said.

"Abhi, stop it!" Deepti said sharply.

"Down!" Abhi said, pointing at his feet.

"What's going on with him?" I asked.

"They taught him opposites," Deepti said, rolling her eyes. "He knows up and down and inside and outside and heavy and light and front and back. The more he knows the crazier he acts."

"You and me both, Abhi," I said, thinking about how I had tried to convince the aunties yesterday with facts and logic, when I really should've pretended that my blood pressure was rising or I was having a heart attack. That's what Hema Aunty does, and they all listen to her.

"Up?" Abhi said.

Deepti groaned, but when she picked him up, she kissed him on the cheek.

"Anyway," she said, "at least we have your Amma and my Appa, right?"

"My Amma's not coming," I said.

"What?"

"She told me she wants to focus on earning the money to pay a bribe for the seat. She said that I shouldn't start this because I'll get a bad reputation and Greenhill will hear about it and won't take me, even if we get the amount we need."

"But you're not listening to her, are you?"

"Of course not."

"Are you telling me that you're disobeying your mother?" Deepti asked. "As in, *your* mother? As in, the aunty that all the other aunties are afraid of because she's the strictest and toughest aunty of all?"

"Yes," I said.

"Isn't she going to kill you? Like, chop you up into little pieces, or lock you in the house until you're dead?"

(No offense, Mrs. Naidu.)

"Probably."

"And Hema Aunty knows you're doing this?"

"She knows I'm doing the SDMC," I said, "but she doesn't know what Amma thinks."

"But still, if Hema Aunty knows, the whole area – including your Amma – will find out in the next ten minutes, if they haven't found out already, right?"

"Probably."

Deepti's eyes got really wide like she was going to say something Deepti-ish – actually, I think maybe even *she* thought she was going to say something Deepti-ish. But whatever it was, she changed her mind. Instead, she said, "I'm tired of talking about this."

"Okay," I said.

"Appa gave me ten rupees. Do you want some groundnuts?"

I said yes, because that's the kind of question I like answering.

I miss questions like that.

So we got some hot groundnuts and walked home. It was gray and cloudy and a little rainy, and the nuts were crunchy and hot, and it felt nice to have a ~~best friend~~ friend again.

Even if it wasn't Amir.

And even if my days are numbered.

All the best,
Sarojini

August 6, 2013

Dear Mrs. Naidu,

Honestly, Mrs. Naidu, it's a miracle that I'm writing to you right now. Because for a minute there, Amma was so furious I thought I was going to die she was going to kill me I would end up in your condition.

Yesterday I came home late, partly because I was helping Deepti catch up on everything she's missed in science classes and partly because I was avoiding a certain eyebrow-raising lawyer's house. Amma was already home when I got there, but instead of making dinner like she usually does, she was scrubbing the floor.

When I came through the door, she didn't look at me and she didn't say hello. Instead, she scrubbed faster, and said, "Hema asked if I was going to the meeting at the school after the holiday."

"What holiday?" I asked.

"I asked her, what meeting is that?" Amma said, like she hadn't heard me. "Hema said, the one your daughter is organizing."

"Oh," I said, really quietly, under my breath.

(Except I didn't say "oh," Mrs. Naidu. I said something much worse.)

Amma didn't hear, because she was saying, "I told her I know that can't be true, because I strictly forbade my daughter from wasting her time like that."

I didn't say anything, mostly because the only words I could think of were ones I had learned from Deepti. Which, as you might imagine, Mrs. Naidu, were not the right words for this particular moment.

When I didn't answer, Amma said, "I told you to stop this nonsense."

(She really did say nonsense, Mrs. Naidu. Amma's not like Deepti. Or like me.)

"Sorry," I said, softly.

"Sorry?" Amma asked, finally turning around. Laser beams shot straight out of her eyes and into my growing heart. Or maybe they went into my stomach, because my insides started to feel like they were being fried. "*Sorry?* I didn't tell you to say sorry. I told you to stop. Stop creating trouble. Stop lying. Stop all of it."

As it turns out, Mrs. Naidu, there is a word that was more wrong than any of the words Deepti had taught me. And even though I knew it was the worst possible thing to say, I said it anyway.

"No."

"What?" Amma stood up and punched her hands onto her hips. She's not very tall, Mrs. Naidu – in fact, I'm already taller than her. But when she stood like that, she looked twice my size.

In my whole life, I have never talked back to Amma. I have always done what she asked me to do, because I thought she was always right. But even though I am only twelve, and even though Amma has always taken care of me, and even though I trust her and love her more than anyone in the world, I had to talk back.

Because today, for the first time in my life, Amma was wrong.

"I'm not stopping," I said, my voice growing louder, like someone was slowly turning up the volume dial in my throat. "You're right, my plan might not work. But *your* plan might not work either. What if we don't have the money for the seat? Or what if we get the money and they still don't take me? Plus you're always going with the aunties to yell at officials who ask for bribes. Why is it okay to pay a bribe when it's for me?"

"Are you openly disobeying me?"

"Yes," I said. "Amma, this time I know what I'm talking about. I spoke to Madam and I read the law and I decided –"

"*You* decided?" Amma interrupted, her voice growing along with her height. "You *decided*? You do *not* make the decisions in this house. I do."

"Why?"

"Excuse me?" Amma said, like she couldn't believe that I would say something like that.

(Which, three months ago, I wouldn't have.)

"Why should you make all the decisions? What if you're wrong?"

"I'm your mother. You are my daughter. Daughters listen to their mothers."

"Like you listened to your mother when you married Appa?" I said – well, actually, I screamed.

Remember I told you about the expression, Mrs. Naidu, the one that goes, 'she looked like she'd just been slapped?'

Remember how I told you how Amir looked at the water truck after I said that horrible thing, and how it was worse than he looked after he was slapped?

Well, Amma looked much, much worse than that.

Except she wasn't sad-worse. She was angry-worse.

"Do you get enough to eat?" Amma shouted. "Do you have a roof over your head?"

"You didn't buy this roof! Tariq and Farooq and Tasmiah Aunty did," I yelled back. I kicked the steel pot we keep under the weakest part of the roof. It rattled angrily and sloshed sludgy water all over the places Amma had just scrubbed clean. "And it still leaks, so it's not like it's much of an improvement!"

Amma didn't say anything for a second, and

beneath our loud, hard breathing and the dripping of rain water on the now-pot-less place on the floor we heard shuffling and whispering, like someone was standing right outside. And honestly, Mrs. Naidu, there probably was someone out there, because in our neighbourhood, everybody can hear everything all the time, even when you're talking in a normal voice – which we definitely were not.

Amma pulled me to a back corner of our ~~house~~ room. Her fingers left red marks on my skin.

"I did not raise you to be disrespectful and defiant," she hissed. Even though she was whispering, it still sounded like screaming. "I raised you to be a good daughter."

"I *am* a good daughter," I whisper-screamed back. "I get good grades. I follow your rules. Now, I'm trying to fight for our family. Why can't you trust me?"

"I used to trust you."

"You mean when I listened to everything you said without asking any questions? I'm not like that anymore, Amma. And I'm not stopping."

"You *are* stopping. From now on, you are coming straight to Madam's house after school. No more Child Rights Club. No more Deepti. No more nonsense."

"But Amma –"

"This conversation is over," Amma said, dropping

my wrist. "Now clean up the mess you made and cut the onions for dinner."

Never in my life had I wanted my own room so badly. I wanted to slam a door and then cry into a blanket and then punch the walls. But in our little place, all I could do was put the steel pot back under the leak and scrub the muddy rainwater off the floor and get out the knife and pretend that my eyes stung because of the onions instead of my anger. For a long time, the only sounds were the rhythm of the drip-drip-drip of rain into the pot, and the sizzle of dosas frying on the tava.

Then things got even worse, Mrs. Naidu, because thinking about apartments with doors made me think of a certain ~~former current former~~ friend, which made remember what holiday Amma was talking about.

Friday is Ramzan – or, actually, Tasmiah Aunty said it's Eid-ul-Fitr, and that the month of fasting that comes before is called Ramzan, but Indians are always mixing things up and saying it wrong.

Which means that on Friday, we're going to Amir's place for Eid dinner.

Mixed-up-and-wrong. Sounds like just about everything in my life right now.

All the best,
Sarojini

Dear Mrs. Naidu,

Even though you were a very successful person, and even though you had a love marriage and a huge house and lots of friends and maids and children and dogs and cats, it seems to me that things weren't always easy for you. Like, for example, you were sick a lot. I read that you needed all kinds of surgeries, and that during one surgery you almost died, and that after another surgery you had to be in a wheelchair and the doctors told you that you might never walk again.

But they were wrong. You walked again. And after that, you marched and sailed and danced and ran and probably even would have flown if you could've made yourself a pair of wings.

When they told you that you couldn't walk, Mrs. Naidu, how did you *know* that you would prove them wrong?

No one's told me that I can't walk. But plenty of people have told me plenty of other things I can't do. Here's a list:

1. They think I can't get a seat at Greenhill.
2. They think I can't fix Ambedkar School.

3. They think I can't convene the SDMC.
4. If I do convene the SDMC, they think I can't make it matter.
5. They think I can't stay out of trouble.

If you've been paying attention, Mrs. Naidu, you know all about #1-4.

Maybe you knew about #5 too. Maybe you've been thinking about it this whole time.

But for me, #5 really started today.

The trouble started at the place where trouble always starts: the water truck. Or, at least, the place where we wait for it (the truck, not trouble). Because today, the water truck was late, so Deepti and I stood side by side with our empty drums, half wondering how we'd get to school on time, and half listening to the latest gossip.

"Can you imagine? A Hindu boy and a Muslim girl," Hema Aunty was saying. "They've been going around together this whole time and the parents didn't know."

"My husband thinks the boy will commit suicide," Amina Aunty said.

"She's such a nice girl," Kamala Aunty said. "Doing a degree in home science, you know."

"Two communities are two communities," Hema Aunty said. "It will never happen."

"Unless they elope," Amina Aunty said.

Hema Aunty and Amina Aunty would have started

yelling (not because they were angry, but because they're not used to talking in normal voices like the rest of us), but two things distracted them.

First the water truck pulled up, which means everyone started elbowing and scrambling for a place in the queue.

(I know it sounds rude, Mrs. Naidu, but we were all late for something – making breakfast, taking our baths, getting to school.)

Second, the air turned white and yellow with flashes of lightening.

Except there weren't any clouds, and there wasn't any thunder – unless you count the sound of aunties banging drums together to get to the water truck.

It was Nimisha Aunty who figured out that the lightening wasn't coming from the sky, but from a camera around the neck of a lady wearing red cotton leggings and chunky earrings. Her painted toe nails peeked out from a pair of leather slippers that Deepti and I had seen on sale in the window of the Bata showroom. The woman's hair kept falling in her face, but instead of using her hands to adjust it, she puffed it away with big gasps of air out of her mouth. (At first I thought that was a sign that she was crazy, but then I realized it was because she was concentrating so hard that she didn't want to let go of the camera). She had been standing to the side, but when the truck arrived, she slid into our crowd as quietly as a raincloud.

"Hey!" Nimisha Aunty snapped, drawing herself up close to the photo-taker and getting into her face – or, actually, getting into her shoulder, because Nimisha Aunty was much shorter than her. "What do you think you're doing?"

"Southern Chronicle," the woman said. She put her camera down and held up the plastic ID card she had on a cord around her neck.

"Reporter?" Hema Aunty said, clutching her chest. "Hai Ram!"

Mrs. Naidu, I'm sure you know a lot about reporters. I know that at Dharansana, you kept the protestors quiet specifically so that reporters would write positive things about Indians and negative things about Britishers. And your plan worked. The reporters wrote about how the British beat Indians with lathis, and the people who read the articles started supporting freedom for India. Plus, you were a kind of reporter yourself: you wrote articles for the Bombay Chronicle and Young India about rights and British Raj and home rule.

So I'm very sure you know what reporters are like when they write about revolution.

But, here's the question, Mrs. Naidu. Do you know what they're like when they write about slums?

"You're here to find out how poor and pathetic we are, aren't you?" Amina Aunty said. Then she turned to us and pointed at the reporter and said,

"She's looking for starving children and weeping women tearing their saris apart."

(That's what they're like, Mrs. Naidu.)

"Actually, I'm doing a story on water shortages," the reporter said in Kannada. When she spoke, her words were smooth and exact, like she cut each one perfectly out of glass and polished it a little before she handed it to us.

I hope I speak like that someday.

In Kannada *and* English.

"That's rubbish," Hema Aunty said. "You should write about how that councillor woman promised us roofs and all we got was plastic."

"Or how our children have fevers from the rains and no doctors have come," Amina Aunty joined in. Then she turned to Mary Aunty and said, "You know they set up health camps over behind the old airport? But here, nothing. What, our children are worth less because we earn less?"

"No, no, no – you should write about the hospital waste," Nimisha Aunty said, pointing in the direction of the smelly slush that runs from the back of the hospital straight through our area like a poisonous river. "The children play in it and get rashes and loose motions."

The reporter didn't say anything. She just kept clicking.

To be honest, Mrs. Naidu, I'm not sure what

she was taking pictures of – I mean, doesn't every area have a bunch of angry aunties yelling about something or the other? Doesn't seem like news to me.

Amma says talking to reporters is a waste of time. Even though I disagree with Amma on a lot of things (especially lately), she's right about this.

Maybe ~~when you were alive~~ during the freedom struggle, it was different. After all, it seems like people all over the world were shocked and angry when they found out about how the Britishers hurt so many Indians at Dharasana. But where I live, Indians get hurt and even killed all the time, but nobody seems shocked or angry when they read about it in the paper. It's not exactly other people who are hurting us – it's more the place where we live is doing it, I guess.

Maybe it's easier to feel angry about bad people than about bad places.

Since Deepti thinks everything and everyone is rubbish, I figured she wouldn't be interested in talking either. So I couldn't believe it when she walked up to the journalist, full drums of water on each hip, and said, "You should write about child rights."

And I *really* thought I was imagining it when the reporter bent down on one knee and said, "What was that?" Her voice was kind of squeaky, like she was talking to a smart anganwadi kid, or maybe a not-so-smart puppy.

As you probably know, Mrs. Naidu, this is *not* the way to speak to Deepti.

I held my breath, waiting for the explosion. And it's true that an angry shadow passed across Deepti's face – a shadow that probably only I noticed. But instead of getting sharp, she took a deep breath, like she was calming herself down, and she said, "You should write about child rights. Like how kids are supposed to have rights but we don't."

"Really?" The reporter kind of laughed and patted Deepti on the head.

(Definitely a not-so-smart puppy.)

"You know the Right to Free and Compulsory Education Act of 2009?" Deepti said in English.

(She really did, Mrs. Naidu. I guess she's becoming lawyerly too.)

"It's a law that says we're supposed to have toilets at our school," Deepti said, switching back to Kannada.

(Okay, so maybe not completely lawyerly. But she hadn't said a single bad word yet, which for Deepti was really something.)

"Also our teachers aren't supposed to hit us, but they do," Deepti said. "That seems like something you should put in your paper. That grown ups are hitting kids even though it's against the law."

"That's not news," the reporter said. Only this time, she straightened up and stopped the squeak in her voice. I guess she finally realized she was talking to a person, not a puppy. "Plenty of people wrote articles about a recent government report that says that hardly any schools are compliant with RTE."

(I don't know what 'compliant' means, Mrs. Naidu, but when Deepti and I talked about it later, we decided it must be a fancy English word for saying that the schools aren't doing what they are supposed to do.)

(Which, as the reporter said, is not news at all.)

"But *our* school is news," Deepti said. "We have a Child Rights Club. So you should write about how bad the school is, and then when we fix it, you can write about how great it becomes. I bet no one's written articles like that yet, have they?"

The reporter crossed her arms and raised her eyebrows.

"It's a good idea, I'm telling you," Deepti said. "Ask Sarojini. She's in the Club too."

When I heard my name, I panicked. No one cares if Deepti to talks to a reporter– in fact, everyone expects Deepti to act crazy. Plus Deepti's Amma doesn't know anything about Deepti's life, and she definitely doesn't have time to read the newspaper. But *my* Amma? Not only does she have spies everywhere, she reads three different newspapers every day, including the

Kannada language edition of the Southern Chronicle. And then, there's the fact that Amma already told me I wasn't allowed to keep trying to fix the school. It's one thing for her to hear it from the aunties. But if she hears it from the aunties *and* reads it in the paper? Or, worse, if Vimala Madam reads it in the paper and Amma hears it from *her*?

Even the most gruesome murder would be nothing compared to my fate.

So I ducked behind Hema Aunty and Nimisha Aunty (who aren't very tall, but luckily, are pretty wide) and tried to hide.

Except, of course, Hema Aunty said, "Sarojini, what's wrong? Go talk to the lady."

And before I knew it, a million rough brown aunty hands were reaching out and shuffling me in front of the reporter.

"You?" The reporter asked. "You're in what, fourth standard?"

"They're Class Six," Mary Aunty said. "And Sarojini is first rank."

"Just because we're poor you think our daughters don't know anything," Hema Aunty said, wagging her finger, which made the fat of her arm jiggle.

"I'm sure these two are very smart," the reporter said. "It's just that I've been reporting on RTE for months, and there are plenty of adults with lots of experience and education and power who haven't been able to get the government to enforce it. It's highly unlikely that a couple of sixth standard girls could do it. That's all I'm saying."

"You people, always putting those pictures of our children looking so sad and hungry on the front page," Amina Aunty said, shaking her head. "But if our children do something right, you don't care. You don't believe it's possible."

The reporter sighed and put her hands back on her camera again. "I'll consider it," she said. But the way she said it made it sound like she had already decided that she wouldn't consider it at all.

Just then, the driver of the water truck started screaming about how everyone better hurry because he was leaving. After a second you couldn't hear him, though, because the aunties started screaming too – at the reporter, who was walking away.

"Ambedkar Government School!" Nimisha Aunty shouted. "Go there and take your big fancy camera."

"Write something positive about our girls for once!" Hema Aunty screeched.

Even Kamala Aunty, who is usually so quiet, kind of half raised her voice and said, "If Sarojini says she'll do it, then she will. She's just like her mother."

Then all the aunties forgot about us and started complaining about Ambedkar School, and how bad the headmaster is and how the hole in the gate has been there forever and how all these low class people are always dumping trash by the compound wall (even though, to be completely honest, Mrs. Naidu, I've dumped trash there, and so has Deepti, and so have all the aunties).

Deepti and I had filled our drums before the commotion, so we were the first to start home. As soon as we got away from hearing distance, I asked, "What were you thinking talking to a reporter like that?"

Deepti shrugged. "Everyone was giving their opinion. Why can't I give mine?"

"If my Amma finds out about this – no, *when* my Amma finds out about this, I'm going to be so, so dead."

(No offense, Mrs. Naidu.)

"Not if we fix the school," Deepti said.

Then she was gone. She moves fast, Mrs. Naidu – with water and reporters.

I don't know what I'm dreading more: seeing Amma's face when she reads in the paper that I'm *still* in the Child Rights Club, or seeing Amir's face when we show up for Ramzan and the two of us have to pretend we're still friends.

If I die, Mrs. Naidu, I hope you and I can meet somewhere and have chai.

All the best,
Sarojini

August 9, 2013

Dear Mrs. Naidu,

One of the reasons I like you so much is because you fought for so many issues that I care about, like girls' education and women's rights. And today I read about something *else* you fought for that I care about: Hindu-Muslim unity.

This book I'm reading says that whenever Hindus and Muslims fought, or there was a chance that they would start fighting, Gandhi Thatha sent you to help everyone stay friendly. It also says that you gave speeches about how one of the best things about Indians is that we have lots of friends who are from different religions and castes and speak different languages. Plus, you knew many Muslims, what with living in Hyderabad and all. It seems like you were close to them because you used to write them letters and go stay with them during holidays and defend them during political meetings, and they used to send you boxes of mangoes and dedicate books to you and have your children over to dinner even if you weren't there.

Based on this evidence, I conclude you went to lots of ~~Ramzans~~ Eid-ul-Fitrs. You probably wore a new sari every time, because you loved saris and shoes and jewellery, and because for most people in India, holidays mean buying something new.

In my house, though, nothing is ever new. Not even on holidays. Everything we own used to be someone else's. Like the bureau, which we got when one of the families Amma works for shifted flats and didn't have space for it any more. Or the cracked mirror, which Vimala Madam was going to throw out until Amma brought it home and stuck it back together with Fevicol. Or my pavade, which used to belong to Tasmiah Aunty's sister's friend's daughter, and which started out too big for me, and now is so tight that I can barely get my arms through the sleeves.

But today, when we went to have ~~Ramzan~~ Eid with Amir's family, for maybe the first time in my life, I got something new: a half sari Tasmiah Aunty stitched on the sewing machine she got from an NGO after completing a tailoring class.

(Tasmiah Aunty didn't actually need the class – she's better than most tailors I know. She only took it because she heard they were giving away all these Singer machines that used to belong to a garment factory.)

(I guess even when you have money, not everything in your house is new.)

Amma and Tasmiah Aunty chased the boys into the hall so I could go into the bedroom and close the door and fasten the clasps on the kumkum-red blouse and tie the skirt around my waist and pin the embroidered dupatta on my shoulder. Even though Tasmiah Aunty hadn't seen me for months, she knew my measurements somehow, and everything fit perfectly, like one of her hugs.

Then I opened the door and twirled around, and the mirrors on the skirt clinked together like the cymbals Kamala Aunty's son plays when she sings bhajans, and everyone commented on how tall I had grown (which is not true because I haven't grown much since fifth standard) and how the deep red Tasmiah Aunty had chosen was perfect for my skin (which is true because everyone knows red goes best with dark skin) and how thin I look (which is not true but everyone says it to kids on holidays so we'll eat more).

Then Tasmiah Aunty and Amma went to the kitchen and Farooq and Tariq went to watch the cricket game on the TV in the hall.

And Amir and I were alone.

"Hi," he said.

"Hi," I said.

Silence.

And not the good kind of silence, which is filled with things you want to say.

The kind of silence that's scratchy with things you *don't* want to say.

After a while, Amir asked, "How's Child Rights Club?" I was pretty sure he was less interested in Child Rights Club and more interested in chasing away the quiet.

"It's good. Right now it's just me and Deepti."

"Who's Deepti?"

"She's my friend."

"The skinny girl from the construction site?" he asked. "She goes around with that little boy?"

"That's her brother," I said. "Abhi."

"Abhi," Amir repeated. He nodded, and then looked at me like it was my turn to say something.

But what could I say?

I didn't want to ask Amir about school, because talking about Greenhill would remind me how I'll never get a seat there, and how I'm never going to be able to fix Ambedkar School, no matter how hard I try. I didn't want to ask Amir about his brothers, because it would remind me of what Farooq said the last time I saw him. And I didn't want to ask Amir about his friends, because it would remind me of how we used to be best friends, but probably aren't any more.

So instead I asked, "Have you gone to Gangarams lately?"

"Not really. I've been studying a lot. But as soon as exams are done, Farooq said he'd take me."

"But exams are in September. That's ages away."

Amir shrugged. "School's really hard," he said.

"Oh."

Silence again.

Then Amir asked, "How's Vimala Madam? Still an evil genius?"

"She's definitely still a genius," I said, "but she might not actually be evil."

"Really?"

"Kind of. She's been helping me with Child Rights Club."

"Wow!" Amir said, laughing.

"I know! She's teaching me about laws."

"I bet your Amma is breaking millions of coconuts."

"Not exactly," I said, looking down at my skirt and playing with the mirrors, which picked up bits and pieces of light and tossed them up on the pukka ceiling.

"Doesn't she want you to be a lawyer anymore?" Amir asked.

"I think she just wants me to live in a nice house."

"Detectives live in nice houses."

"I guess," I said, following where the mirrors were throwing their light. Then, suddenly, I noticed the new sofa that was still in its plastic and the flat screen TV with the cricket game on it and the kitchen that had a sink that filled with water every time you turned a metal switch.

Amir looked at me hard for a second, like he knew what I was thinking, which I thought he probably did.

Except he didn't.

"I'm sorry Amma got you those clothes," he said. "I told her you wouldn't like getting gifts from us, but she said I was being silly."

"What are you talking about?"

"Just," he said, staring at his feet, "what happened at the water truck."

"You mean the charity backpack?"

Suddenly, I felt sad and angry and hurt and all kinds of other things I had never felt around Amir before.

But what was I supposed to do, Mrs. Naidu?

If I told Amir how I felt, it might ruin our friendship forever.

If I pretended nothing was wrong, we would still be friends on the surface, but deep down, we would be strangers.

Then I started thinking about how even though everybody talks about your fate like it's written just for you, you always end up spreading it around, especially to the people you love. Like, for example, how Amma took on extra work because it was written that I needed to pay a bribe if I wanted to go to Ambedkar School. Or how Deepti keeps changing schools because it was written that her parents needed to come to Bangalore if they wanted to keep the family farm. Or how Amir might not have any friends because it was written that his brothers would get good jobs and would want to spend their extra money on switching Amir to a private school.

Then I started thinking about the other kind of fate – the kind we write ourselves, like Deepti thinks we do. And I started thinking about how what we think are good decisions sometimes turn out badly. Like how Amma married Appa and had me, and how Appa left us, and how now Amma can't go home. Or how at Eid, we're the only people Tasmiah Aunty invites over, and how it makes me wonder if she has a story like Amma's that I've never heard.

I thought about how no matter who is writing it, life never stops being hard.

And how when life is especially hard, a best friend can make it the smallest bit easier.

Which is why I took a deep breath, and said, "Amir, I need to tell you something."

But I didn't just tell him something, Mrs. Naidu. I told him everything.

I told him about how Amma and I went to Greenhill because I wanted to go to school with my best friend again, and how I'll never get a seat there because they asked Amma to pay a bribe. I told him about Child Rights Club and going to see Vimala Madam and why Amma wasn't breaking any coconuts. I told him about Deepti, and how she spits and rolls her eyes and swears and steals flowers from posh neighbourhoods, but she also listens and understands and stands up for the people she loves more than anyone I've ever known.

I told him how much it hurt when he drew a line in our friendship, even though he didn't mean to. I told him how I didn't know how to act around him now that he has a whole other life I can't afford.

I told him how a homemade blouse from Tasmiah Aunty is different than a charity packet from Tariq's work. I told him how even though it's nice to have new things sometimes, friends are best when they are old and familiar.

Then Amir told *me* everything.

He told me how even though I might think he's rich the kids at his school still think he's poor. He told me how they make fun of where he lives and how he talks and how he's so far behind, especially in English. He told me how at Greenhill, even after his partial scholarship, there's so much else to pay for, like books and field trips and sports equipment, and how sometimes his family has to skip meals or pay rent late just so they can afford Amir's education.

He told me how he doesn't like his new school, but he can't tell his brothers because they worked so hard to put him there. He told me how the teachers don't pay attention to him except to point out how he doesn't speak English properly or how he doesn't have any manners. He told me how it's kind of nice to have taps and ceiling fans and two-wheelers, but it's not that nice.

And he told me that he wants to be friends again.

Then Amma came to say that the sun had set, and it was time to eat.

When we went into the hall, there were so many items spread out in shiny silver vessels on the floor that there was barely room to sit: spicy biryani with whole hard-boiled eggs; korma and curries that dripped red and yellow and orange down our arms; sticky-sweet halwa that clung to the tops of our mouths until we washed it down with the sugary payasa Amma and I had brought. Amma and Aunty watched our plates, and the second there was any empty space, they filled it up with food. We laughed and ate and ate and laughed and then we ate some more.

Afterwards, we drank Aunty's special chai, and we talked about everything and nothing. Farooq and Tariq made fun of me and Amir like they always do, and Tasmiah Aunty and Amma pretended to be upset like they always do, and then they compared how good our marks were, because that's how it works – the youngest ones get the most attention, good and bad. The house smelled like ginger and ghee and friendship.

Before I left, Amir and I looked out the window and saw the skinny, bendy little moon straining and trying its best to give us light. Let me tell you, Mrs. Naidu, it wasn't doing such a bad job, even though it was so thin it looked like if you got close to it, the smallest sigh would blow it away.

I've been sighing a lot lately, but it's been a long time since I looked at the moon. The thing is, though, whether I look at it or not, every night, it shines on me and Amir and Deepti and Annie Miss and Hema Aunty and Vimala Madam and HM Sir and Amma's family in the village and even Appa, wherever he is. It shines on everyone, no matter who they are, or what they do, or where they go to school.

It's kind of like friendship. At least, best friendship.

No matter how long you ignore it, or how far away it is, or how much it shrinks and grows, it's always there.

Shining.

All the best,
Sarojini

August 11, 2013

Dear Mrs. Naidu,

Now that we are best friends again, Amir spoke to Tasmiah Aunty and got permission to come see me in the coconut grove, even though Aunty and Amma both still think Amir's neighbourhood is safer. But anyway, when he got here this afternoon, we didn't even have to discuss where we were going: we put his shiny new bike inside ~~our his old~~ the house, took a couple of idlis, and went straight to the special place.

I didn't expect this, Mrs. Naidu, but Deepti was already there. She was sitting on the ground with her legs tucked up under her and her back against the fallen tree, staring at a mynah bird perched on a branch. The bird was bobbing its head and wagging its tail and chirping and chattering.

I don't know if you've noticed, Mrs. Naidu, but mynah birds can't sit still.

Usually, neither can Deepti.

Except today.

It turns out there are all these quiet parts of Deepti that she usually covers up with noise. Like the way her body strains against the seams of her too-small clothes. Or how the skin below her eyes is puffy and dark like rain clouds. Or the way her face wrinkles with worry when she thinks no one is looking. Or how when she listens to mynah birds, she looks like she only knows the saddest parts of their songs.

But I barely had time to notice. Because as soon as Deepti saw us, she stood up, put her hands on her hips, looked at me, then Amir, then me, then back at Amir, and asked, "Are you the Muslim boy?"

Just like that, all the quiet parts of her disappeared, and the loud parts came back.

"He has a name," I said. "It's Amir."

"I know his name," Deepti said to Amir, even though I was the one who answered.

"I guess you're Deepti," Amir said.

"Are you still being an idiot to Sarojini?" she said.

(Only she didn't say "idiot," Mrs. Naidu. But you probably concluded that already.)

"Deepti!" I said.

"No, I'm not," Amir said. "Are going to be an idiot to me?"

(Mrs. Naidu, this might surprise you, but Amir didn't say "idiot" either. I guess the brochure is right: Greenhill really *does* expand your vocabulary.)

"Amir!" I said.

Deepti looked at me and said, "He's alright."

I rolled my eyes at her, because that's what she

would've done to me. "Be nice," I said, handing her the idlis. "They're covered in masala powder, just like you like them."

"Mmmmph," Deepti said, which may have been 'thank you,' but it was hard to make out because she was shoving idli in her mouth.

Amir sat on the ground where Deepti had been, with his back against the log. When he bent his knees, his trousers crept way up his legs, which stuck out like the back feet of a grasshopper.

I guess Deepti noticed (although she didn't seem to notice that I told her to be nice) because she said, "How come your pants don't fit?"

"Right. Because *your* clothes fit so well," Amir shot back.

"These aren't mine," Deepti said. "I stole them off a clothesline."

"You did?"

"No," Deepti said. Her face broke into a grin. "But I could've."

"She's right," I said, remembering her climbing the star-flower tree. "She definitely could've."

"Is that why you're friends with Sarojini?" Amir asked, as I settled down on the ground next to him. "So when she's a detective, you can bribe her to keep you out of jail?"

"Sarojini wouldn't take a bribe," Deepti said, crossing her arms across her chest. She cocked her hip and started tapping her foot, like our English teacher does when Roshan and Joseph won't stop doing Rajni impressions. "Besides, she's not going to be a detective. She's going to be a lawyer. You should hear her talk."

"Like I talked to that reporter?" I groaned.

"You talked to a reporter?" Amir asked me. "Are you crazy?"

"What's so crazy about that?" said Deepti.

"Last year a reporter asked Meena Aunty if the water at school was making everyone sick. She said yes, which was true. And she said it's been making kids sick for years, which was also true."

"So?"

"*So*," Amir continued, "Meena Aunty got fired. But it's still the same water, and I bet people are still getting sick. Nothing changed."

"Except Meena Aunty doesn't work at the school anymore," I said. "That changed."

"Meena Aunty?" Deepti asked, jumping on the log above us and rocking back and forth on her heels. "The old lady whose eyes don't point the same direction?"

"She used be the ayah," Amir said. Then he looked at me and added, "before she talked to a reporter."

"I didn't actually *say* anything."

Deepti rolled her eyes. "They can't fire us from school."

"I'm not worried about being fired from anything," I said. Then I thought about Amma, and I asked, "Wait, can mothers fire their daughters?"

"*Your* Amma could," Amir said, shivering.

"Okay, calm down," Deepti said. "This is all part of the plan to fix the school."

"The plan we wrote together?" I asked. "Because I remember a bunch of stuff about playgrounds and corporal punishment, but I'm pretty sure we didn't say *anything* about a reporter."

"See, right now, no one is paying attention to us," Deepti said, ignoring me. She jumped down from the log and faced us with her hands crossed in front of her like an army general. "No one wants to come to our meeting, and no one wants to donate anything. But having your picture in the paper? *That* gets people's attention. They love it!"

"The reporter was taking photos that day," I grumbled. "No one seemed too happy about that."

"That's because she was writing some rubbish story that no one cares about," Deepti said. "But who doesn't want to be in a story about schools?"

"You sure know a lot about journalism for someone who's never been a reporter," Amir said.

"I read the paper. I mean, I've read it before. Once or twice."

"We have to read the paper every day," Amir said, sighing. "It's required for Social Studies."

"Oh, right," Deepti said, rolling her eyes. "You go to that fancy school. How much did you pay for your seat?"

"Amir doesn't have a reservation seat," I said. "He has a real seat."

"A scholarship seat," Amir said quickly, "but it still costs a lot of money."

"Okay," Deepti said. "You have a scholarship seat, maybe, but what did the reservation students pay?"

"I don't really talk to them," Amir said.

"Why?" Deepti snarled. "Because you're so much better than them?"

"No." He looked at the ground and started playing with a rock, pounding it against the earth like he was angry at it. "Because they're all tiny – like four and five years old. I *wish* they were older. Then I might have friends in my class."

"Are your classmates now mean to you?" Deepti asked in a voice that made her sound pretty mean herself.

"Mostly they ignore me," he said. "But they're mean to other people who are small or weak or just different. That's not right."

I guess Deepti approved, because she nodded and she uncrossed her arms.

"They sound like a waste of time," she said.

Deepti jumped back on the log and tried to

balance on one foot. She wobbled around crazily like she was about to fall over.

"I could help, you know," Amir said suddenly.

"I'm fine," Deepti said, miraculously recovering her balance and planting both her feet on the log.

"No, not that," Amir said. "I mean with Ambedkar School."

"How can you help if you go to Greenhill?" I asked.

"I don't know," Amir said. "But I used to go to Ambedkar, and you guys are my friends, and you still go there. Plus I like it a lot better than my school. I mean, the students, at least."

"If we fix Ambedkar, maybe you can come back," I said, like I had just thought of it.

(Even though I've been thinking about it all along, Mrs. Naidu.)

(But you knew that already.)

Deepti sucked her teeth loudly. "Don't be ridiculous, Sarojini," she said. "Nobody changes from a private school to a government school."

I looked at Amir, thinking he would disagree. But he didn't.

"She's right," he said.

"Why not?" I asked. "What if we get better teachers and nice equipment and everything?"

"It doesn't matter," Amir said. "Everyone will

think I got kicked out and they'll start gossiping about my family."

"Plus, nobody who goes to a government school becomes rich or successful," Deepti said. "You think your lawyer Madam went to a place like Ambedkar?"

"No," I admitted.

I guess somewhere deep inside of me, I knew that Amir would never leave Greenhill. After all, at first, even *I* wanted to get a seat at Greenhill, not stay at Ambedkar. But I felt another part of me twist a little, like the growing part of my heart wasn't big enough to handle such bad news.

"I don't think you have to be at Ambedkar to help," Deepti said. "I mean, I'm helping, and who knows how much longer I'll be there?"

"What?" I said.

Mrs. Naidu, it's one thing for Amir to leave. I've already handled that. Sort of.

But Deepti too?

When was *that* written?

"Sure," Deepti said, shrugging in that way she does when she's pretending not to care about something she cares about a lot. "When my parents get a new job, who knows where we'll go."

My insides twisted even harder.

I guess my ~~friends~~ best friends noticed, because Deepti hopped onto the ground on one side of me, and Amir slid closer to me on the other side, and they both put their arms around my shoulders.

"It doesn't matter where we live or go to school," Amir said, "we can stay friends."

Deepti hugged me tightly, probably because she's much better at doing things than saying them.

Then I saw them look at each other over the top of my head, and Deepti rolled her eyes and Amir half smiled. It was like they understood each other without saying a thing.

And that's when I realized that even though it's not going the way I thought it would, my plan is actually working.

At least, the part of the plan where Amir and Deepti and I are all ~~friends~~ best friends.

When I realized that, my insides stopped twisting.

They didn't untwist or anything, but at least they held still.

All the best,
Sarojini

Dear Mrs. Naidu,

For a second there, I thought that it was written that my life would pretty much go back to normal, or maybe even better than normal, just because everything was going so well.

Here is the evidence that whoever is writing my life is writing a happy ending:

Amir and Deepti are friends with each other.

They are also friends with me.

Amma is so happy after seeing Tasmiah Aunty that she's forgotten to be angry at me.

That couple the Aunties were talking about have eloped, which is big news, which means they forgot about the reporter and didn't say anything to Amma.

It's Independence Day tomorrow (which you know, because you were there on the first Independence Day in 1947) which means we have a function but no classes.

Deepti found out I don't like dancing, and she convinced the teachers to let the two of us hold flags and march around the back, which is *so* much better than dancing.

Amma said I don't have to come to Vimala

Madam's house if Annie Miss calls to tell her that she's with me.

I didn't have any homework yesterday so Amma said I could go to the special place and read the book about you.

Can you see how I might have concluded that everything was okay, Mrs. Naidu?

Well, I was wrong.

I got to school this morning, and all my luck was gone.

I thought something was strange when I saw Abhi waiting for me at the construction site without Deepti. He was tracing curvy shapes in the dirt. I guess he thought he was writing Kannada letters, because he kept saying, "Ah-ahhh. Ee-eeee. Oo-oooo," like they teach you when you're little. When Deepti's Amma saw me she acted like she knew I was coming, and then thanked me for taking Abhi to school. I pretended like Deepti and I had discussed it – even though we hadn't – and I left before Deepti's Amma could ask questions that I couldn't answer.

It took me longer than usual to get to school – Abhi kept stopping to count things – but when I got there, Deepti was standing in the front, pointing to the big scooter-shaped hole in the gate and talking to someone.

"It's been like this for ages and nobody cares," she was saying.

Can you guess who she was talking to, Mrs. Naidu?

I'll give you three clues:

1. The person Deepti was talking to was wearing fancy chappals that you can see in the window of the Bata showroom.
2. The person Deepti was talking to kept blowing her hair out of her eyes because her hands were busy scribbling in a notebook.
3. The person Deepti was talking to was someone Deepti should not have been talking to at all.

Since you are a genius, Mrs. Naidu, I'm sure you have concluded that Deepti was talking to the reporter from the water truck.

"Oh good. You're here," Deepti said when she saw me. Then she saw her brother, and said, sternly, "Abhi, go to class."

Abhi let go of my hand and flew across the courtyard like a kite in the wind.

"You're the other girl in the Child Rights Club," the reporter said to me, scribbling away. "Sarojini, isn't it?"

"Yes – no – I mean, don't put me in your article," I said.

"This is Rohini," Deepti told me. "You remember her from the water truck, right?"

"Um," I said. Well, actually, I kind of croaked, because when I thought about my face on the front page of newspapers hanging in every tea shop in Bangalore, my throat started to feel more than a little froggy. The headline would probably say, "Child Rights Club Member Fired from Daughterhood by Mother."

At first, thinking of Amma made me shiver. Then it made me remember to be respectful. So I said, "Nice to meet you, Rohini Madam."

"You can just call me Rohini," the reporter said, blowing her hair out of her face again. "Deepti tells me you've been at this school many years?"

"I don't want to be in the paper, Miss," I said.

"You don't have to call me Miss: just Rohini is fine. And don't worry, we can do this all on background."

"That means she won't put your name," Deepti said. "When she puts your name, that's going recorded."

"Going on the record," Rohini ~~Madam~~ ~~Miss~~ Reporter corrected Deepti.

"Which one are you on?" I asked Deepti, even though I already knew.

"The record one," said Deepti. She rolled her eyes, probably because she knew I knew even before I asked.

"So we've seen the gate and the compound wall," Rohini Reporter said, flipping back through the pages of her notebook. "There's no playground or drinking water to be seen. I spoke to Annie Madam about sponsoring the club, and the HM isn't here, but I have his phone number. What else?"

"We have other things we want," Deepti said. "Like we want them to find someone who can help me. Or, I mean, to help kids like me."

" Like you?" Rohini Reporter asked.

"What I mean is, kids who have gone to lots of schools."

Before I knew it, I was saying, "RTE has a section that requires schools to enroll out-of-school kids like Deepti and then help them learn what they missed so they can stay with their proper grade."

(I guess even when the twelve-year-old girl part of me knows to stay out of things, the lawyer part of me doesn't.)

"Do you mean another student?" Rohini Reporter asked. "Or a volunteer?"

"This is all on the backside, right?" I asked.

"On background, yes," Rohini Reporter said, and her mouth turned up a little at the corner. Even though her lips didn't finish smiling, her eyes did.

I stopped for a second to think. But at that point, I had already started talking to her, hadn't I, Mrs. Naidu?

"You were saying?" Rohini Reporter said gently, her pen hovering above her notebook, ready to start moving again.

So I told her how it wasn't supposed to be a volunteer helping Deepti, but a real teacher. And I told her about how corporal punishment is illegal and how Annie Miss said that teachers needed regular training so they knew how to keep order without hitting us, but they couldn't because they were always leaving school to do election duty or censuses or whatever, unless they bribed people to get them out of it. And I told her about how we were trying to convene a School Development Management Committee, (which Rohini Reporter understood even though I used English lawyer words in between the normal Kannada ones) but the Aunties work a lot, and how even if they stayed home, they wouldn't spend time on an SDMC because they think anything that has to do with the government is useless. Then I told her about our old HM and how great she was, and how the new HM wasn't stopping us, but he wasn't helping either.

"That was some excellent background," Rohini Reporter said. "Are you sure you don't want to go on the record?"

"No, Ma'am," I said. "Um, I mean no, Miss. I mean – no. Just, no."

Finally, she put the notebook in her handbag – which, by the way, I think I've seen in the window of the fancy handbag shop next to the Bata showroom – and actually pushed her hair out of her face with her hands.

"When is this going to be in the papers?" Deepti asked.

"I don't know if it *will* be," Rohini Reporter said. "I came here on my own time because I was impressed with you two. I've never heard kids pitch a story quite so convincingly. I figured if you two were as clever as you seemed, it was probably worth investigating. And after I've spoken to you and seen the school, I want to write about it even more."

"But I don't understand," I said. "All that sounds good."

"It is good. What's not good is that my editor doesn't know that I want to write about this yet. When I tell him, there's a good chance he won't let me."

"What?" Deepti asked. "Why not?"

"It's sad, but Ambedkar is a lot like every other government school," Rohini Reporter said. "Which means newspapers have published a million stories like yours already – especially in the spring, when everyone was talking about that report that said that no one is following RTE. For my editor to let me write this, I have to come up with something new. The story has to be different."

"It's going to be different because we're going to make the government do what it's supposed to do," Deepti said. "Not like all those other people at other schools."

"Are you sure?" Rohini Reporter asked. I know it sounds mean, Mrs. Naidu, but it was kind of soft. Like she didn't want us to lose our hopes, but she didn't want us to get them too high either. "You're smart girls. But you've got to face a lot of adults who don't care if you succeed. Some of them might even want you to fail."

"The aunties believe in us," Deepti said.

"The same aunties who won't join the SDMC?"

Even Deepti didn't know what to say to that.

Rohini Reporter reached into her bag and pulled out a card. It had her name and phone number on it, and fancy curly letters that said Southern Chronicle in English and Kannada.

"If something happens, call me."

She held the card out, and Deepti grabbed it.

"I'll call," Deepti said, "and Sarojini will talk."

"You really have a way with words, Sarojini," Rohini Reporter told me, nodding. "Have you ever thought about becoming a reporter?"

"She's going to be a lawyer," said Deepti.

"How do you know?" I said.

"It is written," Deepti said, keeping her face serious and tracing a finger across my forehead, like she was reading Sanskrit or something.

I was going to smack Deepti, but before I could, Rohini Reporter asked how to get to the main road. Deepti wanted to go check on Abhi before class started, so I said I'd walk her there. We left the school compound and I helped her find her scooter. She put on her helmet (which is bright red, like her leggings) and thanked me and put her key in the ignition so she could drive away.

Just as Rohini Reporter's scooter was spluttering and puttering itself on, I felt my heart drop straight through my stomach and into my feet.

Because right then, Hema Aunty came round the corner to buy vegetables from the cart on the main road. The one by Janaki Madam's house that always has the good spinach.

Hema Aunty looked at me.

Then she looked at Rohini Reporter driving away.

Then she looked at me again.

She didn't say anything, but she shook her head and stuck her big meaty fists into her hips.

I ran back to school and almost crashed into Deepti.

"I'm doomed!"

"What do you mean?" Deepti asked.

"Hema Aunty saw me talking to the reporter woman," I groaned. "I'm so dead."

(No offense, Mrs. Naidu.)

"Things were going too well," I said to Deepti. "I should've known it would be written like this."

"Don't be silly," Deepti snapped. "No one's written anything."

"You just said it was written that I was going to become a lawyer!"

"Yeah, because *you're* writing it that way. You get all excited about this law stuff even when it's boring."

"I'll never be a lawyer." I dropped my face into my hands and squeezed my eyes really tight, like if I closed them hard enough everything would go away. "I'll never get to go to law school or even finish primary school because Amma's going to lock me in the house for the rest of my life."

"Why are you always so afraid?" Deepti asked.

"How come you're never afraid?"

Deepti shrugged and said, "I don't have time."

(Honestly, Mrs. Naidu, if Deepti had been alive when you were alive, she definitely would've been a freedom fighter. Maybe she would've been the youngest freedom fighter in history.)

(But don't worry, you'd still be the youngest person to top the entrance exam to Madras University – I don't think even Deepti is smart enough to do that.)

All the best,
Sarojini

August 15, 2013

Dear Mrs. Naidu,

Happy Independence Day!

Thank you, Mrs. Naidu, for fighting for our freedom. I hope that wherever you are, you are celebrating right now.

Hema Aunty would say that India's independence was written.

Deepti would say people like you wrote it that way.

Me, I think maybe it's a combination of both. It's like Deepti said, I'm writing the part about me possibly becoming a lawyer. But then I didn't write the parts where Appa left or Amma never completed sixth standard or Deepti's parents had to move to Bangalore to try and keep their farm.

I guess maybe it's easier to accept what's already been written if you know that you can rewrite some of it along the way.

As for my fate – well, that still hasn't been written, by me or anyone else. Amma is working so many houses that when she got home last night, she could barely keep her eyes open long enough to eat a few dosas and interrogate me about my homework before she fell asleep.

("Interrogate" is a lawyer word *and* a detective word. It means to ask someone a lot of questions, but in a scary way. It's something that evil geniuses, policemen, and mothers are really good at.)

And since Amma's working so hard, she didn't have time to come to the Independence Day function, which is good because Hema Aunty – who always complains about being busy, but also always has time to be anywhere that there might be gossip – was there telling everyone she saw me talking to a reporter.

Since we had the function today, we didn't have any homework, which means I got more time to read about you. Today, I read about how in the 1930s, you wrote and then passed out all these pamphlets trying to educate Indians about the Britishers and to get people to support the freedom movement. You weren't the only one – it seems like lots of other Freedom Fighters wrote them too – but since you were a poetess, I'm pretty sure yours were the best.

There's one you wrote that's addressed to girls. I'm not sure if you remember this exact leaflet, but it's kind of like a poem.

My favourite lines go like this:

"Do not think of yourselves as small girls. You are the powerful Durgas in disguise. You shall sing the Nationalist songs wherever you go. You shall cut the chain of bondage. And free your country. Forget about the earth. You shall move the skies."

What did you mean by that, Mrs. Naidu?

Here's what I think you meant: I think you meant that even if you're small, like me and Deepti and Amir (even though Amir's not a girl), you shouldn't be afraid to try and make big changes.

But here's the thing, Mrs. Naidu. We *are* trying.

But no one believes in us the way you believed in the people of India.

Here is the list of people who don't think we can do it:

1. Amma
2. Rohini Reporter
3. Headmaster Sir
4. Hema Aunty
5. Nimisha Aunty
6. Kamala Aunty
7. Amina Aunty
8. Mary Aunty
9. Anyone who has spoken to #4-8 on this list.

Here is the list of people who think we can do it:

1. Vimala Madam – but we all know that Madam ~~is~~ might be an evil genius, so it's hard to trust her opinion.
2. Annie Miss – but then, she once said that even if we can't fix our school, the struggle

will still be a valuable learning experience, which sounds like the kind of thing she read in her just-and-beautiful-world books but maybe isn't true in real life.

That's a lot more people thinking we can't do it than people thinking we can.

Then there's the fact that the people who don't believe in us make really good points. Especially Amma.

What if doing this ruins my reputation? What if Amma sacrifices and sacrifices and then I lose the seat because of what I've done?

Or what if I end up staying at Ambedkar School and no matter how much we fix it, it doesn't get better and Amma has to spend her whole life washing dishes because I never get a good education and then never get a good job? What if Rohini Reporter starts writing about Ambedkar School and the government ends up closing it down, like the HM's old school? Then instead of helping the school, I would've made things much worse.

I think you know what I mean, Mrs. Naidu, because the first Independence Day should've been one of the happiest days in India's history, but ended up being one of the saddest. That's because India got broken up into two countries, and everyone forgot about Hindu-Muslim unity and started hurting each other. Tasmiah Aunty's grandparents crossed into

Pakistan then, but her Amma and Appa stayed in India and moved south, to Bangalore. They never heard from her grandparents again. Tasmiah Aunty still sounds sad when she talks about it. And that happened to lots of people, Mrs. Naidu, not just Tasmiah Aunty.

So when you moved the sky, and people became free, they also became sad and scared and angry, even though that's not what you or Gandhiji or any of the other freedom fighters wanted.

When there's so many people and possibilities dragging you down, Mrs. Naidu, it's hard to feel like a Durga in disguise.

How do you forget the earth when it's always beneath your feet?

And when no one wants to help you, how do you move the skies?

All the best,
Sarojini

August 19, 2013

Dear Mrs. Naidu,

Mrs. Naidu, I don't want to alarm you, but I think you should know: this might be the last letter I ever write to anyone.

Honestly, by tomorrow, I might be ~~dead~~ in your condition.

I guess I should explain.

As usual, I stopped by the construction site this morning before school. Abhi had a newspaper in his hand and was waving it around, and Deepti was trying to take it from him. When she finally got it out of his hands he started crying, so she tore off a piece from the back and gave it to him. He held it up and pretended he was reading it out loud, but really he was just saying lots of nonsense.

"Look," Deepti said, shoving the non-torn part of the newspaper at me.

"At what?" I said.

But then I saw it.

An article on page four.

An article by a certain reporter with Bata showroom slippers and floppy hair.

An article in Kannada so perfect that every word was like a cut and polished piece of glass.

Or maybe more like a knife.

I was going to paste the article here, Mrs. Naidu, but Deepti wouldn't give me a copy, and no way was I going to buy one and leave it in the house for Amma to find. So instead, I will tell you the main points:

Ambedkar School has a lot of stuff wrong with it. (The article has a list.)

This means Ambedkar School is not in compliance with RTE.

This makes Ambedkar School the same as lots of other schools all over India.

Ambedkar School is different because it has a Child Rights Club headed by a sixth standard student named Deepti.

Deepti and the other Child Rights Club member said that they are trying to fix the school, but nobody in the community wants to help them.

After I read this, Mrs. Naidu, I had a lot of questions, most of which involved the kind of language that Amma does not approve of and Deepti uses all the time.

I started with, "How did you get this?"

"Rohini came by this morning and gave it to me," Deepti said, taking Abhi's hand and dragging him into the road, which I guess meant we were going to school.

"You realize my Amma reads this paper every day?"

"So? It never mentions your name."

"Everybody knows that there are only two people in Child Rights Club," I said, "and Rohini Reporter specifically says that she talked to you and one other person. Even if I never said anything, Amma would know it was me."

"So you'd be dead either way," Deepti said.

(No offense, Mrs. Naidu.)

"So?"

"So if you're going to die, aren't you glad you died fighting for justice?"

"You think this is going to get us justice?"

"It can't hurt," Deepti said.

By then we were at school, Mrs. Naidu, and things started getting really crazy.

When we walked into the classroom, we saw Annie Miss, which wasn't strange at all. But what *was* strange is that she wasn't alone. She was talking to Hema Aunty, Nimisha Aunty, Mary Aunty, Amina Aunty – even Kamala Aunty.

"Are you Annie Miss?" Hema Aunty was saying. She had a copy of the Southern Chronicle in her hand and was thrashing it around. It crackled like fireworks.

"Yes, that's me," Miss said. She was sitting at her desk, and she looked like she was glad that there was a huge piece of steel between her and the aunties.

"So you're the one that told the reporter that we wouldn't help our girls?" Nimisha Aunty asked. "You told her that we don't care about our children?"

"How *dare* you," Amina Aunty said in a kind of loud whisper, lunging across the desk so her face was just centimetres from Miss's face.

(So much for protection from the desk.)

Miss gulped loudly.

"No one is more important to us than these children," Hema Aunty boomed, "and nothing is more important to us than getting them educated. How could you say something like this? And to a reporter? A *reporter*?"

"If you would please read the article, I think you'll see –"

"Oh, so now you think we can't *read*?" Amina Aunty barked, snatching the paper out of Hema Aunty's hands and shaking it so the fireworks sounds started again. "I'll read to you right now. You said, 'We have been trying to recruit community members to the school development and management committee, but there has been an unfortunate lack of response.'"

"Yes, well, I didn't mean –"

"Now Amina," Kamala Aunty said, gently

touching Amina Aunty's arm and lowering it. "You know how these reporters are. They twist people's words."

"She's right," Hema Aunty said, shaking her finger so that her arm jiggled. "These reporters cannot be trusted."

"They are always writing about how we can't take care of ourselves or our children," Nimisha Aunty agreed.

"And we gave her so many ideas of things she could write. But did she listen? Of course not!" Amina Aunty said, throwing the paper down on Miss's desk with one final snap-crackle-boom.

"We are poor, not heartless!" Hema Aunty said. Then she turned and saw I had come in with Deepti, and she asked me, "What was that thing you wanted us to come to, Sarojini? The Q-R-S-T?"

"SDMC, Aunty," I said. Or, actually, I squeaked.

"SDMC," Hema Aunty repeated. "We shall have it tomorrow. At three o'clock."

"Oh – why, that's – that's wonderful," Miss said. She was smiling, but I saw that her hands were gripping the side of desk. Hard.

"I'll go tell Amma," Deepti said, and flew out of the room faster than a mynah bird.

"Annie, call that reporter woman," Hema Aunty said, folding her arms across her huge chest. "Tell her about this meeting. And tell her to stop writing all these wrong things about us."

"Of course, Madam," Annie Miss said.

I don't know if anyone in the history of the world has ever called Hema Aunty 'Madam' before, but she liked it. She stuck her chin up and nodded like a queen. Then she turned around and left with a big twirl, like she was wearing a fancy kanjeevaram sari instead of an old, patched up nightie. All the aunties followed her.

Miss fumbled through her purse, and mumbled, "Call the reporter woman." She finally fished out her mobile and dialled.

Which was just great, Mrs. Naidu, because if the aunties didn't tell Amma how I was disobeying her, at least Rohini Reporter could put it in the paper for her to find out.

Terrific.

I wonder if Rohini Reporter writes obituaries.

All the best,
Sarojini

August 20, 2013

Dear Mrs. Naidu,

I'm almost done with the book about you, Mrs. Naidu, and it seems like there were a few things that you did pretty often:

You wrote speeches and poems.

You went to jail.

You presided.

At first, I didn't know what 'presided' meant. I just knew that you did it a lot. You did it at the East African Indian Congress in Kenya, the Indian National Congress in South Africa, and the Indian National Congress here in India.

It seems like when you presided, you made sure that everyone followed the rules and got things done.

If that's what presiding is, Mrs. Naidu, I think I it did today. Except it wasn't in another country or in Delhi or anything. It was here, in Bangalore, at the SDMC meeting.

Hema Aunty, Nimisha Aunty, Amina Aunty, and Kamala Aunty arrived together at five minutes after three. Deepti came at ten minutes after three with her Appa and Abhi. (I was surprised, Mrs. Naidu, because I thought only her Amma would come. And also because it turns out that her Appa isn't useless at all. He's a really nice man, actually.) At fifteen minutes after three, Annie Miss passed out biscuits and said that we were ready to start.

"Um, so," Miss said. (Her voice was kind of shaky – I guess she was still nervous from her encounter with the aunties yesterday.) "So – what should we do first?"

Miss looked at Deepti, and then Deepti looked at me, so I said, "I think first we need to check and make sure that we meet the requirements for the committee. We need nine people, and at least 75% have to parents and at least 50% have to be women."

"We're all women except for him," Hema Aunty said, motioning at Deepti's dad. "And except for you and the girls, we're all parents."

"But there are only eight of us," I said. "Unless you count Abhi."

"1-2-3-4-5-6-7-8-9!" Abhi said.

"Yes, well, um… I think… well technically he's a student at the anganwadi, not the school," Miss said. "So, right, because of that, I – I mean I – I – I don't think he counts."

"Who cares about these rules?" Amina Aunty said.

"Just in case someone checks, we should do it correctly," I said. "Where's Mary Aunty?"

"She's gone to her village," Nimisha Aunty said. "Her sister just had a baby."

"Where's your husband, Kamala?" Amina Aunty asked.

"He won't come," Kamala Aunty said, shaking her head. "He says this is women's business."

"Deepti, can you ask at the construction site?" I asked.

"We tried," Deepti said, rolling her eyes, and glancing over at her Appa, who held Abhi on his lap. Deepti's Appa looked a lot like her, except he smiled more, and had a big moustache. He wore a faded shirt and a lungi, and had an old towel wrapped around his head. "They were afraid they wouldn't get a full day's pay if they came."

"What about Sujatha then?" Hema Aunty said.

"Who?" said Deepti.

"Good idea," Nimisha Aunty said. "Sarojini, ma, go get your Amma."

"Um."

I swallowed hard, trying to think of some excuse besides, "if I go and get her she'll chain me up in the house and throw away the key" or "sure, I'll go do that, if you don't mind planning my funeral."

But it was written, Mrs. Naidu, that I didn't have to.

"Hey, Sujatha, there you are!" Nimisha Aunty said.

I laughed nervously, because I thought Aunty

must be joking. But then I turned around, and there was Amma, standing at the classroom door.

And she wasn't alone.

"Of course I came," Sujatha, also known as my Amma, said. "My daughter is organizing the meeting, isn't she?"

"Who's this?" Kamala Aunty asked.

Can you guess who it was, Mrs. Naidu?

I'll give you three clues:

1. Her glasses and her eyebrows have a hard time staying in the right place.
2. There is a strong chance that she's evil.
3. She is definitely a genius.

Since you're also a genius, Mrs. Naidu, you have probably concluded that I'm talking about Vimala Madam.

"Sarojini darling!" Madam said. When she walked in, everybody stood up, like she was the Prime Minister or something. Annie Miss scrambled to unfold a metal chair. Madam acted like she didn't even notice – which maybe she didn't. She settled on the floor, crossing her legs, and tucking her long kurta around her knees. "It's lovely to see you. Excellent article this morning. The media is such a powerful tool for justice."

"Th-th-thank you, Madam," I said, sounding like Annie Miss with her Post-Traumatic-Aunty-Syndrome.

Deepti's eyebrows shot up, and she let go of her Appa's hand and flashed across the room. "Madam?" she said, holding out her hand, "I'm Deepti."

"Ah, of course! From the newspaper," Vimala Madam said, shaking Deepti's hand hard, like she would with a lawyer. "An honour to meet you, young lady. Fine work you're doing here."

"Are you joining our committee, Madam?" I asked.

"Well, Sarojini, I reviewed the law this morning," Madam said. She took off her glasses and wagged them at me the way Hema Aunty always wags her finger at people. "Apparently the committee can have 'concerned members of the community.' As a concerned member of this community, I would love to be involved – that is, with your permission."

Everyone looked very impressed that someone as important as Vimala Madam was asking me for permission to do anything, let alone stay at this meeting in a dusty classroom about the future of something as unimportant as a government school.

"Of course, Madam," I said, trying to sound respectful and in charge at the same time. "Deepti, is that okay with you?"

"Sure," Deepti said. Her Appa kind of poked her and she cleared her throat and said, "I mean, um, yes Madam."

"Thank you so much, ladies," Vimala Madam

said. She put her glasses back on and ran her hand through her hair. "Let's proceed then, shall we, Sarojini?"

Everyone looked at me, because thanks to Madam, they all thought I was in charge. So I sat down next to Amma and said, "Um, okay, Miss, according to the law, we have enough people to start now, right?"

"Correct," Annie Miss said. She looked hesitantly at the metal chair, like she wanted to put it away, but then she left it out and sat down on the floor. Everyone else did too, and Deepti went back to sit with her Appa. "Girls, do you want to get started with our new business, then?"

Normally this is where Deepti's bossiness would come in handy. But she was too busy staring at Vimala Madam like she was a cinema villain.

So it was up to me to start presiding.

Maybe you can tell me if I did it right?

I started by telling everyone that every school in India is supposed to have a management committee. The committee has a lot of duties, like making sure that the budget is spent properly and that out-of-school children get registered, and checking to see if teaching and learning is really happening. But today, we were going to focus on the committee's responsibility to make a school development plan.

I told them about how Deepti and Miss and I had come up with a list of changes that we wanted, and that basically the list was our school development plan right now, because it covered a lot of ways that the school had to improve according to RTE. In case you have forgotten, Mrs. Naidu, here's our list:

1. Repair gate
2. Clean up and repair compound wall
3. Build a playground
4. Get purifiers so we have drinking water
5. Hire someone to help kids like Deepti who haven't been in school for a while
6. Get our teachers training so they can stop using corporal punishment

Then I asked if there were any objections.

"What's an objection?" Amina Aunty asked.

"It's anything you disagree with," I said.

"Well, why didn't you just say that?" Nimisha Aunty asked.

"What, so now my daughter has to use shorter words just because you're only an Eighth Class pass?" Amma said.

"That's three classes more than you, Sujatha," Amina Aunty jumped in.

All the aunties started talking at once. Vimala Madam's eyebrows shot up and she pushed her glasses down her nose.

"Oy!" Deepti said – or, actually shouted.

Then I heard a strange sound that I'm not used to when the aunties are around, especially when someone asks for their opinions. (Because if there's one thing aunties have a lot of, it's opinions.)

You know what the sound was, Mrs. Naidu?

Silence.

"Does anyone disagree with anything?" Deepti asked.

Kamala Aunty said, quietly, "It's a good list, ma."

"Very complete," Amina Aunty said, nodding.

"Actually, it's just a beginning," I said. "The school needs many other improvements, but we thought we'd start with these. Later we can ask for more."

All the aunties nodded and muttered, "Good, good."

(I think Vimala Madam sort of wanted to smile too, because her eyes crinkled even though she had on her evil-genius face, which probably scares all kinds of murderers into confessing when she's in the courtroom. But I bet she can't smile without her face cracking or something, so it's better that she didn't.)

"Then we're all agreed on this list?" Miss asked.

Everyone said yes, so Miss carried on. "What's next, Sarojini?"

(The reason she asked me that, Mrs. Naidu, was because I was presiding.)

"Well, HM Sir said we could do whatever we wanted, so we already have his permission," I said. "But he says he doesn't have any budget, so we have to find the money."

So much for silence, Mrs. Naidu. All the aunties started talking at once. I couldn't tell who was ~~saying~~ shouting what, but they were all basically ~~saying~~ shouting the same thing.

"How can there be no budget?"

"Rubbish – that man hasn't spent a single paisa on this school since he got here!"

"So then where has all that money gone?"

"If he wants to get the funds from *us* he can forget it."

"Janaki Madam would never have stood for this."

"QUIET!" Deepti yelled.

Everyone stopped talking, mostly because they were still shocked that so much noise could come out of such a tiny body. Luckily, I'm used to Deepti, so I started talking right away.

"Some of us need to ask the HM if we can see the school budget," I said. "It's our right as the SDMC. And some of us need to ask someone else from the government for the money just in case."

"The Councillor should give us money," Hema Aunty said. "If she won't fix our roofs, at least she can fix our school."

"Aiyoo, that useless woman?" Nimisha Aunty said.

"Who else are we going to ask, Nimi?" said Hema Aunty.

"If we don't ask, we won't get the money," Amma said.

"Even if we *do* ask this Councillor we won't get the money," Nimisha Aunty said.

"Why did you vote for her, then?" Amina Aunty asked.

And then they were all talking at once again. This time, it would take more than Deepti to stop them. Plus, she had lost the element of surprise (which every good detective knows is the key to solving any case).

"Sarojini, if I may," Madam said, raising her hand.

Vimala Madam was asking me for permission to speak?

Well, *that* got them to be quiet.

(Like I said, Mrs. Naidu: the element of surprise.)

"Yes, Madam," I said, calling on her like I was a ~~teacher~~ presider.

"In my humble experience, it is helpful to enter these meetings knowing exactly how much funding you need," Madam said, "otherwise, you will surely be turned away before you even begin."

It took me a minute to translate what Madam was saying from lawyer language to regular people's language.

"What I think you're saying, Madam, is that we need a budget," I said, slowly.

"Exactly," Vimala Madam said. She leaned back and nodded approvingly, as though I had just topped the Madras University Matriculation Exam, instead of just repeated what she said so it made sense.

All the aunties nodded and murmured. Of course, I think Madam could have proposed running around naked or burning down the school or something and they all would have agreed.

"Sujatha, you should do the budget," Kamala Aunty said. "You're the best with numbers."

Amma didn't say anything, but she straightened up her back a bit. I saw her look sideways at Madam, like she wanted her to notice.

"Amma is the best with numbers," I said. "But she has a lot of work, and this will take some time. Maybe somebody else could draft it and then she could check it?"

"I can start it," Miss said.

"I'll help," Nimisha Aunty said. "I wasn't so bad at maths myself before I got married."

(I don't think getting married changes how good you are at maths, Mrs. Naidu. But that's just how aunties talk.)

After that, the rest of the meeting went pretty quickly. We figured out who would go to the HM and who would go to the Councillor and when our next meeting would be.

"What happened to that reporter woman?" Hema Aunty asked. She looked at Annie Miss. "Did you call her?"

"Yes, I did, of course," Miss said, blushing and fidgeting. "She said she could not come today, but that we should notify her of our progress."

"These people never come when we do something right," Kamala Aunty sighed, "only when something goes wrong."

"Then we better make sure that we do this right," Deepti said.

"Hear, hear!" said Vimala Madam.

Adults are so weird.

(No offense, Mrs. Naidu.)

When we walked out of the school, all the aunties left in a clump, and Deepti and her Appa (who hadn't said anything the whole meeting) took Abhi and went home.

"Excellent work, Sarojini," Madam said, shaking my hand. "This was a very promising beginning."

"Thank you, Madam," I said. "And thank you for coming."

"Sujatha," Vimala Madam said, "thank you for bringing me. Now I want you to know, you can take as much time off to work on this as you would like. Your salary will not suffer. My only request is that you keep me fully up to date. And do let me know how I can be of service."

"Thank you, Madam," Amma said. "But please don't worry. I'll be at your home as usual."

"Your mother is a remarkable woman, Sarojini," Madam said, pushing her glasses up her nose and putting her eyebrow down. "And you, my dear, are a remarkable girl."

"Madam, can I help you find a rickshaw?" Amma asked.

"Nonsense," Madam said. "It's a lovely evening, and I could use the walk. Good night, both of you. Get home safely."

We thanked her, and then she walked in one direction and we walked in another.

There was so much I wanted to ask Amma, Mrs. Naidu. I wanted to know why she came and how Vimala Madam ended up coming with her. I wanted to ask her what she thought of the meeting and whether she thought I was good at presiding. Most of all, I wanted to ask her if she was done being angry with me and had maybe decided to be proud of me instead.

But I didn't get to ask any questions, because all Amma said was, "Go straight home and do your homework. Leave it out for me to check. Then press your uniform and start making dinner."

"Yes, Amma," I said.

We walked quietly for a little while, and then she took my hand and squeezed it. She held it until we got to the corner and she had to go to one of her houses where they were having guests and she was getting some extra money. She pulled me roughly to her, kissed me hard on the top of my head and said, "Be good."

Mrs. Naidu, there are a lot of mysteries in this world.

But none of them are as mysterious as Amma.

All the best,
Sarojini

August 22, 2013

Dear Mrs. Naidu,

Yesterday I read that after India got Independence, you became Governor of Uttar Pradesh. (Well, then it was called the United Provinces of Agra and Oudh.) Before that, you were in the municipal government in Mumbai, and you were the first Indian woman president of the Congress Party. (Annie Besant was a president before you, but she was a Britisher.)

I don't know *exactly* what you did when you held office, Mrs. Naidu.

(When I first read "held office" in this book about you, I pictured you holding Vimala Madam's study in your hands. But then I asked Annie Miss about it, and she says that it means working in the government after a lot of people vote for you to represent them.)

Anyway, like I was saying, based on what I've read, it seems like when you held office, you travelled lots of places and gave lots of speeches and wrote lots of letters to Gandhi Thatha and Nehruji and your family. Also, it seems like the whole time you were trying to make sure that women got their rights and that Muslims and Hindus were united and that the

Britishers left India. Since almost all this happened, I conclude that you were probably very busy, and you were probably also very good at your job.

If you have a second, Mrs. Naidu, maybe you can come speak to our Councillor about holding office. Because I'm not sure what she does, but I don't think it's anything like what you did.

If you remember, at the end of the last meeting, ~~Amma and the aunties~~ the SDMC agreed that we would come up with a budget, and then half of us would go to the HM and half would go to the Councillor. I couldn't believe it, but Nimisha Aunty and Annie Miss had the budget ready the day after the meeting. Amma checked it, and then she asked Deepti to ask the construction people what they thought, because they're always around houses and know what materials cost. Most weren't sure, but a few made a couple of changes. Then Amma checked it again and said it was okay. Even though she's not in the SDMC, Mary Aunty made copies for us at the Xerox store next to the flats where her husband is a night watchman. Amma took two copies and went with Nimisha Aunty, Kamala Aunty, and Deepti to see the HM. Then Annie Miss took two copies and came with me and Hema Aunty and Amina Aunty to see the Councillor, who also happens to be the lady whose face is on the hoarding which is ~~on~~ Hema Aunty's roof.

At first, I thought bringing Hema Aunty was a mistake. The whole time we were walking over there, she wouldn't stop complaining.

"That woman promised me a roof," she grumbled. "Once they get your vote, these people have no thought for anything except power and money. And this year the rains are worse than ever. How am I supposed to keep anything dry?"

"Aiyo, Hema," Amina Aunty finally said. "We're not here about your house. We're here about the school."

"She's right," Miss – who had gotten over her Post Aunty Stress Syndrome – said. "We need to stay focused."

"I'm telling you, that woman will give some excuse," Hema Aunty said. "She's like all the other politicians. Corrupt. Useless. I don't know why we bother asking."

"She might say yes, Aunty," I said. "Not all politicians are bad."

(When I was saying that, Mrs. Naidu, I was thinking of you.)

Hema Aunty clicked her tongue and put her hand protectively on my shoulder. "So sweet, Sarojini. But you're young. You'll see."

(I don't know why adults are always saying that kids don't know anything because we're young. Plenty of grownups don't know anything either.)

"We *should* at least try," Kamala Aunty said. "Who knows?"

"Waste of time," Hema Aunty muttered.

"This is it," Miss said.

'It' was where we were meeting the Councillor, and 'it' wasn't what I expected, Mrs. Naidu. From reading about you and Gandhi Thatha and Panditji and Ambedkarji and Gokhaleji, I thought politicians either lived in huge houses or tiny ashrams, and that they worked in offices piled with papers and plastered with posters for their party and filled with people wearing khadi who want to make India a better country. I thought it would be one of those buildings so full of energy that you could tell from the outside that it was someplace special.

But this place didn't look special at all. It was a set of normal-looking flats on the corner of the main road. The building wasn't posh exactly, but it was much nicer than any of the homes in our area. It had a little garden inside the wrought iron gate and a winding stone staircase that smelled like it had been freshly mopped. The Councillor's flat (which I guess is also her office) was at the top of the stairs. The door was open, and there was a pile of chappals in the hallway.

We all hesitated at the door, except for Hema Aunty, who walked right through and led us into the flat. It was crowded with furniture and dark teak panelling. There were a lot of people sitting on leather couches looking at their cellphones. They were mostly men with big moustaches and fat bellies. No one was talking. There were no stacks of paper, no posters, and no khadi anywhere.

Hema Aunty sucked in her breath. I followed her eyes and saw why.

It was the face on Hema Aunty's roof.

Except instead of floating by itself on a hoarding, it was attached to a woman stretched out on a divan, wearing a nightie, full make-up, and chunky gold jewellery. Her long, choppy hair looked like it had been straightened and dyed at a salon. She was texting on her mobile, but doing it really slowly because her long, polished nails got in the way of pressing the keys.

Without looking up, she said, "Yes?"

I think we were all confused, Mrs. Naidu. Because aren't politicians supposed to care? And aren't they supposed to get dressed properly in the morning? Aren't they supposed to be excited to speak to the people who voted for them?

(I guess maybe that's just you, Mrs. Naidu.)

Annie Miss was the first to recover. She said, "Mrs. Reddy, we're here from the SDMC."

"The what?" Mrs. Reddy asked. She still didn't look up.

"The school," Hema Aunty said loudly.

"Which school?"

"Ambedkar Government School," Amina Aunty repeated, slowly and loudly, like maybe Mrs. Reddy was deaf, or didn't understand Kannada.

"I called yesterday?" Miss said, her voice adding question marks where they didn't belong. "I'm the Class Six teacher? The Child Rights Club sponsor? You said we could come? This morning?"

"I get so many calls," Mrs. Reddy said, waving her hand like she was swatting a mosquito.

"Yes, well," Miss said.

"What is it you want?"

Mrs. Naidu, during monsoon season, when I was young, I used to sit outside our house and watch the wind whip around the branches of the coconut trees in our grove just before it started to rain. Sometimes, eagles would land on the leaves of the trees, I guess because it was hard to fly when the air was so angry. I never understood how it was possible that something as skinny as the frond of a coconut leaf could be tough enough to hold the weight of one or two or even three eagles, especially when the wind was blowing so hard. No matter what, the leaves never fell down, and they never let go.

Those leaves are a little bit like Deepti and Amma and Tasmiah Aunty and probably you, too, Mrs. Naidu – much stronger than they look. It's the kind of strong I want to be one day – the kind that only needs a few skinny twigs to hold up the weight of the world.

That's the kind of tough I thought Mrs. Reddy would be. But she's not like coconut leaves. She's like the monsoon wind, pushing anything and everything out of her path, and not in the least bit interested in protecting anyone from a storm.

Annie Miss was the only one of us who was nice enough to stay polite, so she said, "We're from the school management committee. We've come because our school is not in compliance with RTE – that's the right to education."

"I know what it is," Mrs. Reddy said. She was still staring at her phone but I thought that I saw the corners of her eyes pinch.

"Then you know that our school is in violation of the law," Miss said, "and that as a Councillor, it's your duty to help us fix it." I couldn't believe it, but even Miss's voice was getting the tiniest bit sharp. All the question marks were definitely gone.

"*My* duty?" Mrs. Reddy said.

And then she laughed, a deep, bubbling laugh, like a mother-in-law in a Kannada serial just before she explains her evil intentions.

(Serials are not as good as detective novels, Mrs. Naidu, but sometimes they feel a bit more like real life.)

When she heard that laugh, Hema Aunty had had enough.

"Don't speak to a teacher like that," she snapped. "This woman gives her life to serving our children, which is more than I can say for you. Why do you think we elected you, to just sit on your couch in all your gold and act like you're better than us?"

Mrs. Reddy didn't say anything. She just went back to her phone.

"What Ms. Hema is trying to say," Miss said in her just-and-beautiful-world voice, "is that RTE is based on the idea that the local leaders will work with schools to help improve the education system. And since you're the local leader –"

"That's not what it's based on," Mrs. Reddy told us.

"Yes it is!" Amina Aunty said.

"Sarojini, tell her," Kamala Aunty said, putting her hand on my shoulder.

Then they all looked at me.

Even Mrs. Reddy looked up.

Mrs. Naidu, I know that you've spoken in front of hundreds of people, and that probably some of those people were kings and queens and presidents and prime ministers. And I know that I've never met anyone like that before.

Still, I have a feeling that none of those leaders laughed like Mrs. Reddy.

I straightened my back and cleared my throat and, using my best lawyerly voice, I said, "RTE says that the SDMC is supposed to come up with a development plan. Then we are supposed to present the plan to local leaders and they are supposed to help us implement it."

"So what you're asking for is money," Mrs. Reddy said.

"We brought a copy of the plan with a budget," I said, and handed it to Mrs. Reddy. She put down her phone and looked at it while I kept talking. "We would like either to get a donation from you or to raise the money with your help."

"Hmmm," Mrs. Reddy said. She still didn't look at us, but at least this time her eyes were on the plan instead of her text messages.

She flipped through the pages, and none of us said anything, because I don't think any of us knew what we could possibly say to someone who seemed to care more about the state of her fingernails than the people who voted for her.

Finally, she put the papers down on the table, picked up her mobile, and said, "If I am interested I'll let you know."

The air became heavy and thick with silence.

"Come," Hema Aunty finally said, grabbing Kamala Aunty and Annie Miss by the elbows. "I told you this was a waste of time."

Annie Miss said, "Thank you," over her shoulder, as Hema Aunty dragged her and Kamala Aunty out the door.

I guess at first they didn't notice that they had left me behind. Mrs. Reddy was still looking at her phone. "Ma'am," I said, "why did you become a Councillor?"

She paused for a minute like she was deciding whether or not I was worth speaking to. I guess she decided I was, because she looked at me with her smile that looked stuck on her face with Fevicol. "Why do you ask?"

"I'm reading a book about a female leader now," I said. "She cared a lot about girls and their education. I was hoping you would be like her."

(Obviously, Mrs. Naidu, the female leader I am talking about is you.)

Mrs. Reddy kind of snorted and went back to punching the buttons on her phone. "What was your name again, child?"

"Sarojini," I said.

Mrs. Reddy said, "When you get older, you'll understand."

"I don't think so," I said. "I don't think I'll ever understand people like you."

"Like me?" Mrs. Reddy asked. She sounded like she was about to laugh again. "And what am I like?"

"I don't know. But I know who you're *not* like. You're not like any of the aunties who came with me today."

"Are you saying that you'd rather be like one of those women than like me?" Mrs. Reddy said, putting her phone down and staring me.

"Definitely," I said.

I don't think she understood, Mrs. Naidu, but I wasn't going to stay and explain it to her. I left, and when I got outside, Hema Aunty stopped yelling and wagging her finger long enough to put her arm around me and roughly pull me close.

"Useless woman," she said, kissing me on the top of my head so hard that a bunch of curls sprung loose from my plaits.

"Forget her," Amina Aunty spat. "We'll find another way."

I'm not sure if we will, Mrs. Naidu. But at least I don't feel so alone any more.

All the best,
Sarojini

August 23, 2013

Dear Mrs. Naidu,

I'm very sorry, but this letter will be short. I'm sitting in Vimala Madam's kitchen (don't worry, she's not here, she's in her study) and Amma thinks I'm doing my social studies homework which I'll definitely do later, but honestly, Mrs. Naidu, how can I be expected to concentrate on anything until I tell you what's going on?

Since you fought for many kinds of freedom in many different countries for many different people, you probably already know what I'm about to tell you. The visit to the HM went just as badly as our visit to the Councillor. Deepti said that he wasn't at school (which is obvious because it's not the first of the month yet) but Amma figured out where he lived, so they went to his house (which is also obvious, because once my Amma decides she's going to do something, nothing stops her from getting it done). Deepti said that the HM asked them to speak to the Block Education Officer, so Amma got his number and called him in front of the HM. She said the BEO told her to speak to the HM, and then Amma said that if they were so confused about who was in charge of the budget, they should probably speak to each other. Then she handed the phone to the HM.

Apparently both the HM and the BEO got upset and told Amma that she couldn't just go around demanding financial information like that. Then Amma said that actually, she could, because one of her responsibilities as an SDMC member was to monitor spending – which, if you think about it, Mrs. Naidu, is a very lawyerly thing to say. I guess the HM was not impressed, though, because he told her something that I can't repeat here but was very rude and then Amma said she was going to call a famous human rights lawyer and tell her that the school was breaking the law. And when she was done with that, she said, she was going to call the Southern Chronicle and make sure they ran a terrible article about the school on the front page.

"So basically, there was a lot of yelling," Deepti told me, "but no budget."

When I talked to Amma about this last night, I asked her if she thought maybe the HM and the BEO were taking money or selling rations or doing any of the other things you read about schools doing in the paper. Amma told me that it's possible, but she thinks it's more likely that they wouldn't give her a budget because they hadn't made one, and they were embarrassed about it. She says she wants to ask Janaki Madam, the old HM, for advice. But she says that even if there is a budget, requesting money is going to take a long time, so we should try and start with someone who can give us the money right away.

So that's a long way of saying that we may have a plan and a committee, but that's pretty much all we have, Mrs. Naidu. And you can't build a playground with a sheet of paper. (Unless that sheet of paper is a cheque. Which, in our case, it is not.)

I saw Amir this afternoon. He came by Ambedkar School on his bike just as Deepti and Abhi and I were leaving, and then he got off his bike and walked us to the corner where Deepti had to turn left and I had to turn right and he had to go straight.

"Is there anyone else we can ask for donations?" I asked.

"Amir, don't you have any rich friends?" Deepti asked.

"I don't have any friends, remember?" he said. "Except you two. Are either of you rich?"

"I *have* lived in a lot of fancy houses," said Deepti.

"I never thought of it that way," I said. "You've actually lived in some of the poshest places in Bangalore. Probably even posher than some of the houses of Amir's non-friends."

"Yeah, Deepti," Amir laughed. "Can't you get your fancy house people to help?"

Then Deepti got this funny look on her face, and she said, "My people," kind of under her breath.

"Deepti," I said, "whatever you are thinking, please stop."

Then she said, "Bye," and turned left a whole two blocks earlier than she had to.

"What's she up to?" Amir asked.

"Trust me, the less we know, the better," I said.

Amir shrugged and said, "Hey, do you want to come over?"

"I can't," I said. "Amma basically told me that if I don't come straight to Madam's house after school she's going to send me away to a convent in Bihar."

"They take Hindu girls in convents in Bihar?" Amir asked.

"I don't know," I said, "but you know how my Amma is. She makes impossible things happen all the time."

Amir and I paused for second, thinking about my Amma and all the things she could do to me. Then Amir said, "Well, now that you're not fighting, maybe your Amma will make the school development plan happen too."

I hope he's right, Mrs. Naidu. Because lately it feels like every time we solve a problem, twice as many take its place.

I better start my social studies homework now,

Mrs. Naidu. I think Amma is getting suspicious, and even with all its problems, I like Bangalore a lot better than Bihar.

All the best,
Sarojini

August 24, 2013

Dear Mrs. Naidu,

Mrs. Naidu, today proved that I should be a lawyer and not a detective.

There was a case to solve today, and I missed all the clues.

If this were detective story, it would be called the Mystery of the Missing Deepti.

Here are the clues I missed:

1. Deepti was not at the construction site today. Neither was her Appa.

2. But when I got to school, I saw Abhi at the anganwadi.

3. Even though Abhi was there, Deepti did not come to school until just before lunch.

4. When she came to school, she sat across the room and didn't even look at me.

5. At lunch, she left again, and didn't come back until the middle of the afternoon.

6. When she came back, the tips of her fingers were bright blue.

7. She still didn't sit next to me or look at me.

8. Before the end of the day, she left one more time, and didn't come back.

As you can see, Mrs. Naidu, there were a lot of clues. But instead of examining the evidence and drawing conclusions, I was just confused.

I solved the mystery at the same time as everybody else: at the end of the day, when school was over, and we all rushed across the compound and towards the gate to go home or to buy candy or to run around the streets until our parents called us for dinner.

But when we got to the compound wall, we all stopped. Because we all saw the most important clue at the same time:

People were fixing the compound wall.

Can you guess who was fixing it, Mrs. Naidu?

(Since you are a genius, I bet you can.)

It was Deepti and her people.

And by her people, I mean the construction people.

They were picking up garbage and putting it in bags and then taking it to the trash area by the construction site.

They were sweeping the stones where the garbage was cleared.

They were laying bricks on the jagged, broken parts of the wall until it looked straight and smooth.

They were even painting the wall.

Deepti was helping, adding layers of blue paint with a thick, new paintbrush.

Which explains why her fingers were blue.

(You see what I mean about my detective skills?)

"How did you do this?" I asked her.

"I did what Amir said," she said. "I talked to my people."

Deepti's Appa came over then. Beaming, he asked, "What do you think, Sarojini?"

I looked at the fresh bricks and the gleaming paint and the swept stones. I smelled the air that no longer seemed rotten. "It's beautiful."

And it was, Mrs. Naidu. It really was.

All the bricks were laid perfectly. The wall was only partly painted, but the bright blue made it look like a piece of the afternoon sky.

"Where did you get the bricks and paint and everything?"

"A few days ago we ran out of supplies and some of the men had to go to a store and get some," Deepti said. "Appa and I went over there to talk to the man who owns it. Turns out he went to Ambedkar School and said he could donate. He doesn't have a big store or anything, and it's not like he's rich enough to give a lot, but he gave what he could."

Just then Amir pulled up on his bike. He looked at me, and he looked at Deepti, and he looked at the students and the construction workers, and he looked at the soil underneath where the garbage used to be. Without even asking what was going on, he said, "We have extra paint at my house.

And I'll bring some clippings from Amma's terrace garden."

Then he biked away.

That's the thing about Amir. He just understands.

And he always wants to help.

That's when I looked around and noticed that Amir wasn't the only one who wanted to help. My classmates weren't standing and watching, like I was.

They were picking up garbage and painting the wall and passing bricks and mixing sand and water to make mortar.

"Aren't you going to get in trouble for missing work, Uncle?" I asked Deepti's Appa.

"We spoke to the foreman yesterday," he said. "He wasn't happy, but he said he wouldn't fire us. We're going to lose a day's wages, that's all."

"Isn't that a lot?" I asked him.

"Deepti's Amma is working," Deepti's Appa said. "We'll manage on that. Anyway, this is more important than a few rotis, isn't it?"

Deepti smiled then, but I guess she was embarrassed, because she turned back to the wall and started painting faster.

"You should be proud, Sarojini," he went on. "You are the reason that this is happening. My daughter brought us here today, but you are the one who started it all."

That's when I stopped to check what I was feeling.

I realized that I *wasn't* proud.

I was angry.

Really angry.

Why should Deepti's Appa and all the other workers have to miss a whole day of wages for something the government should be doing for free?

Why should kids who are supposed to be doing their homework spend their afternoon picking up garbage?

And why should shopkeepers from the neighbourhood – people who may have a little more than me or Deepti, but still don't very have much – give up supplies and materials that they could have sold to make money to feed their families?

"Excuse me, Uncle," I said. "There's something I have to do."

I went back to Annie Miss's classroom then, Mrs. Naidu. She was pretty much the only teacher who was still at school. First I told her what was happening outside, and then I asked if I could use her phone. She wanted to know who I was calling, but when I told her, her eyes got that misty-just-and-beautiful-world-look. She handed me the phone, and told me not to worry about using minutes.

She said that equity is worth more than a few extra rupees on her phone bill.

(I don't know what that means, Mrs. Naidu, but it was nice of her.)

Then she went down to the compound wall to see if she could help.

The first call I made was to Rohini ~~Madam Miss~~ Reporter. She picked up after just one ring. When she answered, I said, "Hello, this is Sarojini from Ambedkar School."

"Tell me, Sarojini," Rohini Reporter said.

"Are you free to come to the school?" I asked. "Because I think our story just became news."

"Hold on, hold on," Rohini Reporter said. Then I heard a bunch of shuffling, and the sound of her blowing her hair out of her eyes, and then she repeated, "Tell me."

As I was talking, she kept saying, "yes, yes, and then?" In the background, I could hear the scratch-scratch-scratching of her pen on her notebook, the click and whizz of cameras, and the metallic sounds of voices speaking over microphones.

When I finished, I asked, "Where are you, Ma'am – um, I mean, Miss – I mean –"

"Actually," she said, "I'm at a press conference in your area. I'm with a lot of reporters."

"Is Mrs. Reddy there?" I asked.

"In fact," Rohini Reporter said, "she is."

"Please tell Mrs. Reddy and your reporter friends that if they would like to come to the school right now, they are very welcome," I said.

"How kind of you, Sarojini," Rohini Reporter said. "We're on our way." I could hear her smiling through the phone.

The second call I made was to Amma.

"Sarojini?" Amma asked. "What's wrong?"

"Amma, I'm not coming to Madam's house today."

Amma listened without interrupting while I told her about the construction workers and Deepti and her Appa getting supplies donated and Amir getting paint and Rohini Reporter coming to write about what was happening.

"I'm going to talk to the reporter when she comes, Amma."

"Talking to a reporter? Why?"

"Because the media is a powerful tool for justice."

(Like I said, I might be a lousy detective, but I'm a pretty good lawyer.)

"Sarojini, these reporters are useless, and –" Amma started.

"And because it's not fair," I said, interrupting my Amma for maybe the first time in my life. "Why should kids pick up garbage and parents lose wages when the government is supposed to do all this? Why is everyone always trying to take things away from the people who don't have very much to begin with?"

Amma sighed, and then she said, "If I knew that, kanna, I wouldn't be breaking my back every day."

We were both quiet then, Mrs. Naidu. Because sometimes, you understand someone better after just a couple of words than you do after a lifetime of conversations.

"I'm going to call Hema and ask her to be with you," Amma said.

"Why?" I asked. "Don't you trust me?"

"Of course I trust you," Amma said. "And I know Hema Aunty can be brash and sometimes say sharp things. But she would do anything to protect you – you and all the other kids from our area."

"I can do this myself, Amma."

"I know you can. But you shouldn't have to."

After I hung up, I went down to the wall to return Miss's phone, and everything happened at once. Amir showed up with brushes in his pocket and buckets of sky-blue paint looped around his handlebars and cuttings in his bicycle basket. Then Hema Aunty came with Kamala Aunty and Amina Aunty, even though I'm pretty sure Amma only called Hema Aunty. Kamala Aunty started picking up garbage, Amina Aunty got a group of kids together to plant cuttings in the soil where the garbage had been, and Hema Aunty started ordering people around, which I guess was her idea of helping. Then Rohini Reporter came with journalists from two TV stations and three newspapers.

As you might have guessed, Mrs. Naidu, Mrs. Reddy was not with them.

But that was okay, because there were plenty of other people for the reporters to interview instead.

First they interviewed Annie Miss, and she explained about our Child Rights Club.

Then they interviewed Deepti and her Appa. Deepti did most of the talking, and her Appa mostly just nodded and smiled shyly underneath his bushy moustache.

Then they interviewed Hema Aunty, because she said they had to, and she screamed a lot, but if you listened to the actual words she was saying, a lot of it made sense.

Then they interviewed me. I told them about how we were sick of being ignored by the Councillor and the HM and the Block Education Officer and everyone else who was supposed to help us with our school.

"Why do you need the government to intervene?" one of the reporters asked me.

"We don't need them," I said. "Just because we're poor doesn't mean that we don't know how to take care of ourselves."

"Then can't you just do this yourselves?" another reporter asked.

"Of course we can do it ourselves," I said. "But we shouldn't have to."

That was the quote that Rohini Reporter put in her story, which came out on Sunday afternoon, and which Amir and Deepti and I read out loud together in the special place.

Rohini Reporter also wrote about how while this was going on, Mrs. Reddy held a press conference where she lit a lamp to start an initiative for adolescent girls. When Rohini Reporter asked what Mrs. Reddy was doing about RTE considering what was happening at Ambedkar School, she said something about being dedicated to education. But the way Rohini Reporter wrote it, you could tell she thought Mrs. Reddy was acting pretty silly.

"I never thought I'd ever say this, but Hema Aunty is right," Amir said. "That Councillor is completely useless."

"At least the wall finally looks normal now," Deepti said. "You know Hema Aunty's son, Roshan? And Joseph, Mary Aunty's son? They said that if we could get more colours, they can paint pictures on the wall. They're pretty good, too – I've seen them drawing comics when they're supposed to be working."

"You guys got Roshan and Joseph to work?" Amir

shook his head. "Wow. Now *that* deserves a story in the paper."

"Front page," Deepti agreed. And we all laughed.

"Do you think Mrs. Reddy read this?" I asked, tapping the newspaper.

"I hope so," Deepti said, tearing especially fiercely into the dosa I brought her from home, "and I hope she feels terrible."

"I doubt it," I said, shaking my head.

"I wish we could get Greenhill into the paper," Amir said. "I heard this kid in my class saying that the last time there was a bad article everyone went crazy and fixed the problem immediately."

"What bad article are they going to write?" I asked. "The halls are too shiny? The equipment is too new?"

"Um, hello?" Deepti said. "This is the school that tried to bribe you and your Amma for a free seat, and you can't think of a bad article?"

"I can't talk to a reporter about that."

"Why not?" Deepti asked.

I looked at Amir then, thinking he would help me, but he looked like he agreed with Deepti.

"If nobody talks about it, then the school will keep doing it," Amir said.

"But even if I did speak to the papers about the bribe, how does that help Ambedkar School?" I asked.

I'm not sure what Deepti and Amir said after that, Mrs. Naidu, because the inside of my head was too noisy.

Because at that moment, I realized *exactly* how speaking to the papers could help Ambedkar School.

All the best,
Sarojini

August 28, 2013

Dear Mrs. Naidu,

A day or two after I last wrote to you I went to Vimala Madam's house after school. Not because I had to, but because I wanted to.

(I know, Mrs. Naidu. Things get weirder and weirder.)

It turns out Madam wanted to see me as well. When Amma answered the door, she said, "Go straight to the study."

"Am I in trouble?" I asked.

"Did you do something wrong?"

(Which you'll notice, Mrs. Naidu, was not an answer.)

"No," I said.

"Then?" Amma said. "Go quickly. She's very busy."

So I straightened my skirt and patted down some of the curls that had come loose from my plaits (although I don't know why, Mrs. Naidu, considering who I was going to see) and I knocked on the big, heavy wooden door.

The voice inside ~~called~~ barked, "Come."

I pushed open the door, and Madam was sitting

behind her desk, her glasses on the edge of her nose, her eyebrow raised, her hair puffed up in black and gray storm clouds.

When she saw me, she pushed her glasses up and her eyebrows down. Which I appreciated, because at least she was trying to be normal.

"Another excellent story in the papers, Sarojini," Madam said. She had the English language version of the Southern Chronicle on her desk. She picked it up and said, "You gave such a wonderful quote. Brilliant."

"Thank you, Madam," I said. "But actually, I was just repeating what Amma said."

"I am not surprised," Madam said. "It takes a smart woman to raise a smart daughter like you."

"Yes, Madam," I said.

"So, now that you have the world's attention, what's next?" She leaned back in her chair and crossed her arms in front of her chest. Her glasses slid down again, even though she didn't touch them.

(I guess at this point, they're trained to move straight to the end of her nose.)

"The thing is," I said, sitting down stiffly, "even though we have used the media as a powerful tool, we still don't have justice. Or, actually, we still don't have money."

"Justice, money," Vimala Madam said, waving

her hands in the air. "It all amounts to the same thing."

I have no idea what that meant, Mrs. Naidu. But I said, "Yes, Madam," because I think that's what she was expecting me to say.

"This is a serious dilemma, Sarojini," Madam said, in that voice she uses for lawyers and kids. "Do you have any ideas?"

"I think I might. I spoke to Annie Miss – that's our teacher –"

"I met her," Vimala Madam said, nodding. "Lovely woman. Very committed."

"Right – um, I mean, yes Madam. I spoke to her and the anganwadi Miss, because the anganwadi Miss has lots of stuff at the centre, like plastic chairs and a stove and all these picture books. Anyway, they said that politicians don't really give money. They usually give things. Like the person who was the Councillor before Mrs. Reddy gave the anganwadi Miss the chairs and the stove and everything."

"I see," Madam said, nodding.

"But we want a playground, and I don't think the Councillor would donate something as big as that," I continued. "I mean, actually, I don't think she'll donate anything. And the HM wouldn't give Amma a budget, so we don't know how much money the school has. Or, actually, we don't know if the school has *any* money."

"Your Amma mentioned," Madam nodded.

(I was a little surprised by that, Mrs. Naidu – if you've noticed, Amma doesn't exactly talk much, especially about what she calls "our problems.")

"So based on all this evidence, it seems like we need to ask someone else for money for the playground," I said.

Madam didn't say anything, but she put the palms of her hands together and kind of leaned her nose into them and nodded, just like an evil genius would do right before she told you her plot to assassinate the queen.

(At this point I'm mostly sure that Vimala Madam isn't evil. But when she does stuff like that, I still have my doubts.)

"At first I didn't know what to do, considering that the government is supposed to give us money. But then I thought of someone I could ask for the money," I said. "Or some place, actually."

I stopped for a second, not sure how to tell her my idea.

"So?" Vimala Madam asked.

I know that when you read it here, it sounds like a question, Mrs. Naidu. But you know how Vimala Madam is: she can even make a question sound like a command.

So I told her about my breakthrough.

I told her about how after I learned about the 25%

reservations in Child Rights Club, Amma took me to Greenhill. (I didn't tell her about how I wanted to get a seat at Greenhill because ~~my best friend~~ one of my two best friends goes there. But that's not really an important part of the defense, is it?) Then I told her how the secretary at Greenhill had asked Amma for a bribe.

"That's when I came to you with the pamphlet about the law and you explained it to me, Madam," I said. "And then I talked about it with Deepti and we got the idea to fix our school."

(I didn't tell her the part about how I thought ~~my best friend~~ one of my two best friends might come back if the school was fixed. Because that's not really an important part of the defense either, is it?)

The whole time I was talking, Madam's glasses were getting lower and lower and her eyebrows were getting higher and higher. If I hadn't stopped, I think she may have run out of nose space. She definitely would have run out of forehead.

"Sarojini, I'm very disappointed," she said. "I have mentioned to you numerous times that I am a human rights lawyer with extensive experience. Furthermore, I am the founder of one of the foremost child rights NGOs in India. My organization and I would have been more than happy to take your case regarding the corruption you faced when you were only trying to exercise your right to a reservation seat under the 25% quota."

When I heard that, my stomach began to twist. "I didn't want to trouble you, Madam," I said, looking down at my lap. "I didn't think I should bother you with something this small."

"Small?" Madam ~~asked~~ barked, smacking her desk with her hand. "*Small?* Children all over Bangalore are facing the same situation that you find yourself in because schools like Greenhill are unwilling to fulfill their responsibility under the law. Each instance like yours sets a dangerous example. Challenging just one case could alter the course of history. Why, with a defendant as likeable and intelligent as you, we would surely win a stunning victory. Your case could change the lives of children all over this city – perhaps all over this great nation! This case is *not* small. Not at all. In fact, it is enormous!"

By now she was yelling. It wasn't like the aunties yell at each other over small things just to be dramatic, or like Amma yells at me when she wants to protect me. It was like yelling at an imaginary judge and an imaginary courtroom that was full of imaginary reporters ready to use the media as a powerful tool for justice.

(I don't yell very much, Mrs. Naidu. But if I did, I'd want to yell like that.)

"I'm sorry, Madam," I said. "But when we went over the law that first time, I thought you were trying to get me to understand that it was more important to fix the government schools than to get into the private schools. Because I'm not sure how much 25% is, but it seems like a lot less than the number of people who won't get reservations. That's all I meant by small."

Madam stared at me and my stomach twisted harder. She didn't move or make a sound for what felt like a long time. Then, all of a sudden, she sniffed and looked off into the distance, absently tapping her fingers on the desk.

"I suppose that *was* what I was trying to communicate," Madam said. Or, actually, she kind of grumbled.

She kept staring for a while. Then, finally, she cleared her throat and looked at me again.

"Well, what do you have in mind, Sarojini?"

So I told her, Mrs. Naidu. And when I did, she actually smiled.

I'm not lying.

She *smiled*.

And her face didn't crack and her head didn't explode and the universe didn't crumble into pieces.

(I don't know, Mrs. Naidu – what happens when an evil genius smiles?)

And then she walked across the floor and past my chair and opened the door and yelled into the kitchen, "Sujatha! With your permission, I would like to take Sarojini on an educational excursion tomorrow morning. You can let the school know that she will miss her morning class in order to receive some training that will be vital to her future legal career."

(Which was just a fancy way of telling Amma that Vimala Madam is taking me to Greenhill tomorrow to execute our plan.)

(I don't know why she couldn't just say that, Mrs. Naidu.)

Being a lawyer might be more interesting than being a detective, Mrs. Naidu. But that doesn't mean I don't like detective stories. Do you remember my favourite part of detective stories?

The suspense.

(Don't worry, Mrs. Naidu – by tomorrow, you'll know everything.)

All the best,
Sarojini

August 29, 2013

Dear Mrs. Naidu,

Are you ready for me to end the suspense, Mrs. Naidu?

I'll tell you this: the story I'm about to tell you has a happy ending.

You know why?

It leads to a happy beginning.

Sort of like the beginning of free India.

~~Except smaller~~.

Except different.

This morning I got to Vimala Madam's house early so we could go to Greenhill in a car with a driver and A/C and everything. When I got into the back seat, I wanted to look out the window and wave at everyone so they could see how stylish I've become.

But, as usual, Madam had other ideas.

"Sarojini, today you will be asking for justice from an institution that is unsympathetic to your cause," she said. "In order to succeed, you must be adequately prepared."

(Translated from fancy lawyer language, this means: the people at Greenhill are mean, so make sure you have the right words.)

(But since you are a genius, Mrs. Naidu, you probably understood that already.)

It only takes twenty minutes to walk to the school, but in Bangalore morning traffic, driving took almost an hour. The whole time Vimala Madam asked me questions she thought that the HM of Greenhill would ask me. When I answered, she would nod, and then ask *more* questions that sometimes got harder, and sometimes just made me think.

She'd ask things like, "Is there a more precise way to say that?"

Or, "What evidence do you have to make this claim?"

Or, "How do you think the HM will respond to what you've just said?"

I have to say, by the time I got to Greenhill, I felt a warm, cottony confidence curl up inside my chest. My stomach stayed perfectly still, even when we walked through the shiny white halls and passed the trophies and photographs, and when I saw my face reflected back at me a thousand times in all the mirrors and glass.

Until we got to the main office.

There, at the desk, was the secretary who had asked Amma for a bribe.

I felt the confidence leap up my throat and try to force its way out of my mouth. It must've been stepping on my guts, too, because my stomach started to twist and turn.

It's funny, Mrs. Naidu. Even though I remembered her, the secretary didn't remember me. When we walked up to her, she didn't say anything at all.

Then again, maybe she would've remembered me if she had actually looked at my face, instead of leaping out of her chair and falling all over Vimala Madam.

"Madam Vimala Rao!" she screeched, clapping her hands together. "*So* lovely to see you. It's been far too long. How are your darling children?"

"They're doing just fine, Nilofer, thank you," Vimala Madam said. "Sarojini and I have an appointment with the Headmistress. Could you please let her know we have arrived?"

"Yes, of course, Madam," the secretary said. And even though Madam had just said my name, the secretary didn't even glance at me. "Please come, please come."

Without any questions or problems or embarrassment, Madam and I walked right into the place that Amma and I had tried so hard to talk our way into, months and months ago: behind the maze of desks and bureaus, through (yet another) polished glass door, and into the headmistress's office.

"Mrs. Rao!" the headmistress said. "What a wonderful surprise!"

If the secretary was all hard and sharp and shiny, the headmistress was all soft and smooth and round. Her short hair curled into ringlets around the dimples in her chubby, milk-tea-colored cheeks. She was wrapped in a cotton-silk sari that was the same purplish-pink as the bottoms of clouds at sunset. Instead of shaking Vimala Madam's hand, she gave her an enormous hug.

"How lovely to see you," she beamed. "Sit, sit."

"Always a pleasure to see you as well, Padmini." Vimala Madam settled into the chair across the desk from the HM like it was a big fluffy sofa instead of a stubborn piece of teak. She motioned for me to sit in the chair next to her. I tried to lean back at first, but ended up perching on the end of it like a mynah bird getting ready to fly.

"Nilofer, would you fetch us some tea?" the headmistress said to the secretary. "Thank you, darling."

"If you don't mind, I'd like Nilofer to stay," Madam said.

"Certainly," the headmistress said. The secretary smiled her glittery smile, and I shivered. "And who is this?"

"This is Sarojini," Vimala Madam said. "A brilliant young woman with a great deal of potential. Top rank, excellent character – someday she'll make a fine lawyer. Already she has proven to be a leader in her school and community. She and her mother are like family to me."

I looked over at the secretary and I thought her face flickered a bit at the edges. Maybe she remembered me after all.

"I see," the headmistress said, winking at me. "We at Greenhill try our best to support young leaders like you, Sarojini. Especially girls."

I looked over at Vimala Madam, who nodded at me. I took a deep breath and said, "Actually, Madam, I'm here because I tried to get your support a few months ago."

"Oh?" the headmistress said.

"My Amma and I came to see if I could get admissions here," I said. "We tried to get a place under the 25% reservations."

This time the secretary's face flashed all the way across, not just at the edges. She definitely remembered me now.

I told the headmistress everything, just like Vimala Madam and I practiced – or, at least, almost everything. I told her about how I didn't know the rules to RTE when I came here last time, but now I did. I told her how if they hadn't filled their UKG and LKG classes they should've given me a chance, instead of dismissing me. I told her how they had accused us of bringing a false income certificate, which wasn't fair, and also wasn't true.

Then I had to say the hardest thing of all. I gulped and looked sideways at Vimala Madam. And she was doing that thing, Mrs. Naidu – actually all of those things. She was leaning back in her chair and crossing her arms in front of her chest. Her eyebrows were way up her forehead and her glasses were way down her nose and her eyes were focusing all her evil genius power on one person.

The secretary.

Who, by now, was an odd shade of white-green, like she couldn't decide whether to faint or throw up.

Based on the evidence, I concluded that the best thing to do was to finish the story fast, before Vimala Madam's eyes melted the secretary into a puddle. "The thing is," I said, swallowing, "they also asked us to pay a bribe for a seat."

"Excuse me?" The headmistress sat up straighter, and pulled her soft features into something hard and stern. "Young lady, that is a very serious accusation."

"And one that she can fully substantiate," Vimala Madam said in her Vimala Madam voice that is impossible to respond to if you are kid.

But not if you are a headmistress.

"Mrs. Rao," the headmistress said, shifting in her seat and adjusting the perfectly creased pallu of her sari. "We are one of Bangalore's most reputable institutions. We have educated generations of leaders. We stand for –"

"What exactly has been your progress with filling the seats designated for 25% reservations?" Vimala Madam interrupted.

"We are finishing the paperwork to allow us to declare ourselves a minority school," the headmistress said, sticking her nose in the air.

"A minority school?" Madam ~~asked~~ barked. "On what basis?"

"We serve a sizeable number of Muslim and Christian students –"

"Yes, I noticed that your newsletter mentioned that you took in quite a few minority students this year," Vimala Madam said. "Convenient, isn't it?"

"The parents and alumni were fully in favour of this action," the headmistress said. Then she sighed, and added, "Mrs. Rao, you know that I am the staunchest supporter of this law, and that I do my best to take in scholarship students whenever I can."

(*Partial* scholarship, I thought to myself, remembering Amir.)

"The fact is that RTE itself is flawed," she continued. "We cannot maintain our record of excellence if we enroll students with no guarantee that the government will reimburse us for precious time and resources. And, if – and here I stress *if* –

they reimburse us, the amount they're quoting won't even begin to cover our costs."

"That's a poor excuse," Vimala Madam snorted.

(Which made me feel bad for the HM, Mrs. Naidu, because it sounded like the she didn't really like what she was doing, but couldn't come up with another solution. But then I remembered how the secretary had looked at me and Amma like we were diseased, and how Deepti was treated at St. Augustina, and how Deepti and I had found our own solution, even though we're just kids. When I thought about all of that, I didn't feel bad for her at all.)

Then the headmistress turned to me. "Sarojini, is it?"

"Yes, Madam," I said.

"Sarojini, darling, I know you must be upset, but you can't go around accusing people of bribery just because you didn't get a seat."

"Pardon me, Mrs. Headmistress, Ma'am," I said. "But I'm not accusing anyone of anything. It really happened. Amma and I were both witnesses. I also have this." I reached into my bag and pulled out the piece of paper where the secretary had written down the bribe. I held it up so she could see it.

(I didn't hand it to her, Mrs. Naidu, because I knew from detective novels that criminals always try to steal evidence, so you have to keep it close.)

"Why Nilofer," the headmistress said after a moment, "I do believe this is *your* handwriting."

I looked over at the secretary and she had gone from white-green to green-green. But she was also slumped against the wall and her legs were shaking, so the fainting/vomiting chances were still fifty-fifty, as far as I could tell.

"I've recently been working with some reporters to help draw attention to the problems with RTE," I said, going back to the script Vimala Madam and I had rehearsed.

The headmistress was silent, which took me a minute to realize, because she was staring at the secretary, and the anger in her eyes crackled like the air before a thunderstorm.

"At first, I thought I would tell them about this bribe," I said a bit louder, trying to drown out all the static. "I think it could draw attention to all the problems kids like me are having getting seats. But then I realized that I don't *want* a seat at Greenhill any more. What I really want is for my school – my *government* school – to be better."

The headmistress's eyes cleared a little bit, and she said, "Go on."

"So then I was thinking: What if Greenhill generously donated a playground for Ambedkar School?" I reached into my bag one more time and pulled out the budget the SDMC had written. "The cost is almost the same as the bribe."

"It's quite a bit more than that," the headmistress said, looking at the budget. She took out a pen and scribbled the numbers on a sheet of paper, like she was double-checking the total. (Which, by the way, is something that Amma could do in her head.)

"It might be," I admitted. "But it's definitely not more than the cost of fighting a lawsuit from a famous human rights lawyer who almost never loses."

Vimala Madam raised one eyebrow and sort of nodded.

Mrs. Naidu, there are many things I cannot do.

I can't raise one eyebrow.

I can't shove specs down my nose. (Mostly because I don't own specs.)

I can't make the air crackle.

But you know what I *can* do?

I can find the right words.

Because after the headmistress finished her calculations, she looked up at me and said, "A donation of this size certainly could be arranged. In fact," she continued, leaning back and chewing on the end of the pencil absently, "this could be an excellent lesson to our students, not to mention a demonstration of Greenhill's commitment to our community."

"Brilliant!" Vimala Madam said, slapping the desk again. "I do believe we should arrange for a press conference."

"Yes, indeed," the headmistress said. "What school did you say you went to, Sarojini?"

"Ambedkar Government School, Ma'am."

"Ah yes," she said. "We have a student who came from there this year."

"Amir," I said.

"You know him?"

"He's my best friend," I said. "Well, one of my best friends." After a second, I added, "Madam."

"I see," the headmistress said. "He's a lovely boy. So polite. Just like you. And actually, he was in here the other day with one of his teachers asking about starting a tuition program for out-of-school students. You wouldn't know anything about that, would you?"

"He hasn't mentioned anything," I said, smiling quietly, "but it sounds like something he would do."

"Hmmm," the headmistress said. She made a note in a register on her desk, and said, "I'll call your headmaster and formalize the arrangements. Both for the press conference and the donation. As for the tuition program, we'll have to see."

"Yes Madam," I said.

"Sarojini," Vimala Madam said, "I trust you will call your media connections?"

"Yes, Madam," I said.

"And I trust that you, Padmini, will address the issue of bribery with your staff."

I looked over at the secretary again. Her eyes glittered like a trapped cat's.

"You can be sure of it, Mrs. Rao," the headmistress said. Then she reached out and took my hand. "I am so sorry that this happened to you at our school, Sarojini. Thank you for coming to me so we could make it right."

Then Vimala Madam said a few lawyerly things and mentioned how she would love to attend the next board meeting and some other stuff that I didn't hear. Then she and I left.

And it was done.

Madam drove me to Ambedkar School. I couldn't wait to run inside and tell Annie Miss to call Rohini Reporter and to convene an SDMC meeting and to tell Deepti and Amir that after all the fighting and failing and fighting and failing, finally, we had stopped failing.

(Don't get me wrong, Mrs. Naidu. I know there's lots more fighting and failing in our future. But it's a lot easier to fight when you have a non-failure in your past.)

As I was getting out of the car, Vimala Madam shook my hand.

"I am more and more impressed with you, my

dear," she said. "Please know that in all things, you have my full support."

(Which I think is Vimala Madam's fancy lawyer way of saying that she wants to help me always, and not just now, and not just because we're working on this together.)

(I don't know why she couldn't just say it like that, Mrs. Naidu.)

"Thank you, Madam," I said.

"Mark my words, darling. This is only the beginning."

I hope she's right, Mrs. Naidu.

Because the best endings are the ones that lead to new beginnings.

But I guess you already know that, Mrs. Naidu. Because I learned that from you.

All the best,
Sarojini

September 2, 2013

Dear Mrs. Naidu,

Well, Mrs. Naidu, I'm happy to say that even though the secretary of Greenhill may be dishonest, the headmistress is not. She called our HM to arrange the donation and the press conference, just like she said she would. It's lucky that she called today, because if you remember, usually, our HM only comes in on the first of the month. But this month, the first was a Sunday, so he came in today, which is the second.

Deepti and I didn't know anything about Greenhill calling until almost the end of English class. It seemed like any other day. English Miss came late, as usual, and then she put a bunch of sentences on the board and told us to copy them on our slates, as usual. Then she got out a stack of Kannada language magazines and started reading them and not paying attention to us.

(You would think that since she's the English teacher, she'd read English magazines, but she never does. The only time she *doesn't* read Kannada magazines is when she has other work to do. Then she doesn't put sentences on the board and she makes us help her.)

(Once we put address stickers on all of her daughter's wedding invitations. Even though it took us two whole classes to finish, and even though the mandapam was across the street from the school, she didn't ask any of us to come.)

Deepti and I worked together on copying the sentences down. We kept going up to Miss to have her check our work and to read what we were writing out loud to see if we got the pronunciation right. We were the only ones though – nobody else was paying attention. Miss didn't seem to care, even when the talking got kind of loud. I guess her magazine was pretty interesting.

So it was basically a normal day in class, until Roshan and Joseph started acting out their favourite scene from the latest Rajni film.

In case you don't know who Ranjnikanth, Superstar is, he's a famous Tamil cinema action hero. The reason he is popular here is because he's from Bangalore, and he started out as a bus conductor. I think that's why the boys love him: they all think if Rajni can become a star, then so can they. (Well, all the boys except Amir, Mrs. Naidu – but he's not like regular boys. He's much smarter.)

So anyway, whenever those two act out a Rajni scene, it's always the same thing. Roshan jumps around the desks doing these weird karate chop moves that I've never seen in any films, but that Joseph swears is a perfect impression. Probably because Joseph thinks everything Roshan does is perfect, even when it's dumb. *Especially* when it's dumb.

English Miss was reading her magazine, ignoring all the jumping around, until Roshan got the brilliant idea to launch himself off the old broken metal desk that's been sitting in the back of the room for at least five years now.

(You see what I mean about Amir compared to most boys, Mrs. Naidu?)

He landed right on Joseph, and Joseph fell over and all his books went everywhere and there was a loud crack, which at first we all thought was either Joseph or Roshan, but turned out to be the wooden bench Joseph and a bunch of other kids had been sitting on.

(I wasn't surprised, Mrs. Naidu, considering that these benches are so warped and rotten from rain that even sitting on them makes them buckle and bend.)

Joseph and all the kids hit the floor and slates and chalk pieces flew everywhere.

Well *that* got Miss to pay attention. She jumped up from her desk and grabbed her wooden stick and hit Roshan with it.

"Stop misbehaving, you idiot!" she yelled.

(Only she didn't say "idiot." She said something much worse.)

None of this was that unusual, Mrs. Naidu. Whenever you disturb Miss's reading, she gets out her stick and screams and then she forgets about it.

But then, something unusual happened.

The HM came running through the door.

And *his* Rajnikanth impression was much more believable than Roshan's.

He sailed across the room and, just like an action hero, stopped the stick in midair before it hit Roshan again. He grabbed it out of Miss's hand and yelled, right in her face, "What do you think you're doing to this child?"

The room went silent.

It was the first time in my life I have seen Roshan and Joseph be perfectly still.

"Sir," Miss said, after a minute. "He was disrupting class, and I –"

"Hitting students is illegal," the HM barked. He backed away, but kept the stick. He held it tightly in front of him when he spoke, and I got the feeling that he could use it to do some Superstar moves if he needed to.

"But Sir," Miss said, laughing nervously. "If we don't use the stick, the students will not respect us."

"Earn their respect," the HM said. He looked at the sentences on the board and picked up my slate. He kind of threw the slate back down on my bench. "Show them you actually care about your job."

"And if they misbehave?" Miss asked. She kept smiling, like she was trying to make the HM think she was joking, even though we all knew she wasn't.

"It's called positive discipline, and you should've studied it in your B.Ed. program. Anyway, you and the other teachers will be attending training on it later this month," the HM said. "You'll get plenty of ideas then."

Deepti and I looked at each other. Deepti's mouth dropped open, and I think mine probably did too.

Do you know why, Mrs. Naidu?

Training about corporal punishment was an item on our school improvement plan!

"Until then," the HM said, leaning close to her and growling, "I suggest you keep the students occupied by actually *teaching*."

Deepti turned bright red and covered her mouth. I stared down at my slate so I wouldn't start laughing looking at her.

"Deepti, Sarojini," the HM barked. "I need to see you in my office. Now."

Remember how I said that the HM looked like a sidekick? Not any more, Mrs. Naidu.

Now, he looked like a Superstar.

Or maybe an evil genius.

It was hard to tell.

The walk through the school from our classroom to the HM's office never felt so long. I think even

Deepti was nervous, because she grabbed my hand and crushed it between her fingers. She didn't let go.

We finally made it to the HM's office after what seemed like hours (even though it was probably not even a minute). He twirled around and crossed his arms and narrowed his eyes.

"I got a call from the Greenhill Public School headmistress today," he said.

"And?" Deepti asked.

I elbowed her, but the HM didn't seem to notice.

"She tells me she's interested in donating a playground," he said. "She mentioned something about a press conference?"

Then Deepti elbowed *me*. Hard. I turned to look at her and she kind of nodded and raised her eyebrows, which is Deepti for, "Be lawyerly."

I gulped and said in a tiny, squeaky, unlawyer-like voice, "It's an item on the school improvement plan, sir. I went and asked for the donation on behalf of the SDMC."

Sir nodded, but didn't say anything.

"You said not to bother you…" I said, my voice trailing off.

"You'll get full credit at the press conference," Deepti said. "Don't worry. Sarojini is handling the donation, but I'm handling the press stuff."

"Is that right?" Sir asked.

And I can't be sure, Mrs. Naidu, but I think he almost smiled.

"Yeah, I know the reporters around here," Deepti said, like she was a local leader instead of a twelve-year-old girl.

Then the HM really did laugh. But it wasn't a mean laugh. It was kind. And for a second, I thought I saw the face of someone who used to think of his students as his sons and daughters.

"Fix it for the thirteenth," the HM said. "My wife says it's an auspicious day for this kind of thing. And make sure you speak to one of your mothers. They'll know what we need for a lamp-lighting."

"Yes sir," Deepti said, grinning.

We stood there watching him for a second. Then, he seemed to remember where he was. He replaced his grin with a growl, and said, "Get back to class."

"Yes sir," we both said at the same time.

As soon as we left the office, we jumped up and down and squealed.

"Class!" he yelled. Then he put his head around the doorway and waved the stick at us.

"Yes sir," we said, and ran back to class together giggling.

When we got to English, everyone was sitting silently, doing their work. Even Roshan and Joseph. The sentences were still on the board, Miss had unlocked the bureau and was pulling out some workbooks that Janaki Madam bought for the last teacher.

Deepti and I went back to our benches and got out our slates. By the end of the day, we had to sit at opposite sides of the room, because we couldn't look at each other without laughing.

In the book about you, Mrs. Naidu, there's a French saying, '*A chacun son destin*,' which means, 'to each ~~his~~ her own destiny.' Which I think is just another way to say, 'it is written.'

The book says that you never liked that phrase much. So you did what writers do – you found the right words. You read them in a poem, and you started signing your letters that way.

Here are the words you found, Mrs. Naidu:

'*A chacun son infini*'

'To each ~~his~~ her own infinity.'

When we left school today, I asked Annie Miss what infinity is. She says that it's an English word that means going on forever and ever and ever.

That's how my heart felt today, Mrs. Naidu. Like it went on for ever and ever and ever.

I guess my heart really *is* growing.

All the best,
Sarojini

September 13, 2013

Dear Mrs. Naidu,

Today, I went to my very first press conference. I guess you've probably been to a lot of those, Mrs. Naidu, but just in case ~~they changed after you died~~ you've forgotten what they're like, let me tell you what happened.

Even though it is the thirteenth, and not the first, the HM came to school. He brought flowers and a brass lamp that he said used to be his Appa's. He even helped us sweep and clean the classrooms, just like Janaki Madam did before she retired.

Right before lunch, the SDMC members came, and so did the HM from Greenhill. She came with Tasmiah Aunty, Amir, and a bunch of other Greenhill students.

When Vimala Madam greeted the Greenhill HM, I heard them talk about how the glittery secretary had resigned. But I didn't say anything.

When our HM saw Amma, he pulled a folder out of his bag. He opened it and flipped through the pages with her, saying, "Here's the school budget. And here are some notes I made on what the school needs. Talk to that SDMC of yours and see what we can do."

Amma ran her hand down the page, nodding slowly. I could see the numbers adding and subtracting and dividing in her head.

We set up Annie Miss's classroom with lots of paper decorations that Hema Aunty got from the temple after they finished celebrating Krishna Janmashtami last week. Nimisha Aunty set up the lamp and drew rangoli around its bottom in orange chalk she got from the anganwadi Miss. Deepti's Appa poured the oil, and then Kamala Aunty set up the wicks. Hema Aunty and Amina Aunty got all the Ambedkar School girls together and pinned orange and white jasmine flowers to our hair. It made us smell sweet and smoky, like a temple.

Nobody from Ambedkar School talked to anybody from Greenhill, and nobody from Greenhill talked to anybody from Ambedkar. Except Amir, who is from Greenhill, but only spoke to Ambedkar students.

Then a bunch of parents from Ambedkar and Greenhill showed up, and so did the journalists. While everyone was finding seats and setting up cameras, Rohini Reporter came over and hugged me and Deepti, which maybe wasn't very reporter-like, but was definitely very Rohini Reporter-like. I saw the Headmistress of Greenhill watching us, but she didn't say anything.

Then the Headmistress of Greenhill told Amir and the other students to line up behind her. There were five wicks on the lamp. The HMs lit one each, then Annie Miss lit one, and then Amma lit one. The Headmistress of Greenhill asked Vimala Madam to light one, but she handed the match to me and Deepti, so we did it instead.

I saw both HMs watching us, but they didn't say anything.

Then the Headmistress of Greenhill talked on and on in a fluffy-clouds-at-sunset voice about how the board and faculty of the school was committed to helping all children fulfill their potential, regardless of their economic status, and how it was their privilege to break ground on a playground today. As she spoke, she kept readjusting her purple silk sari, which was much fancier than anything anyone else was wearing, but that she would probably give to her maid in another year or two.

Our HM and Vimala Madam spoke then, but they didn't take as long as the Headmistress of Greenhill. Madam seemed annoyed, like she wanted Annie Miss and me and Deepti to speak instead of her, but luckily we didn't have to.

Then the reporters asked questions. Usually this scares me, but today, every time I got nervous I looked at Rohini Reporter and she smiled and blew her hair out of her face and nodded so her chunky plastic earrings danced around her cheeks, and I felt better.

Just as the questions were ending, the click of cameras flashing and whisper of pens scribbling was drowned out by a thuk-thuk-thuk-thuk rattle-rattle-rattle-rattle sound. Some of the Ambedkar School students ran to the door, and Roshan called out, "Someone's here!"

Can you guess who it was, Mrs. Naidu?

I'll give you three clues.

1. She was wearing enough gold to pay for all the roofs in the coconut grove.
2. She was staring at her phone.
3. She had nails as long as tiger claws.

By now, you have probably concluded that it was Mrs. Reddy, the local Councillor.

But even though she lived only a few blocks away from the school, she wasn't walking.

And she wasn't alone.

She came in a rickshaw.

Actually, she came in three rickshaws. She sat in one, and two rickshaws chugged along behind her, which explained the thuk-thuk-thuk-thuk.

The second rickshaw was full of water purifiers, which explained the rattle-rattle-rattle.

The third rickshaw held three brand new toilets, which didn't explain anything at all.

And even though the press conference was over, and nobody had invited Mrs. Reddy, and nobody had asked for toilets, and all the wicks of the lamp had been lit, and all the photos had been taken, Mrs. Reddy started speaking into the cameras like it was part of the agenda the whole time.

Which I guess explains why she was wearing a sari instead of a nightie.

"I'd like to thank all the generous people at Greenhill Public for supporting our humble little school," Mrs. Reddy said in English, even though everyone else had spoken in Kannada. Someone came up behind her (he must've been in the rickshaw with her – or maybe underneath the toilets) and handed her a garland. She placed it around the Greenhill Headmistress's neck.

I think the Headmistress was confused, but her eyes stayed round and soft, and her smile stayed wide and dimpled.

"In my own small way, I also want to make a contribution," Mrs. Reddy swept her arm out, so that her sari flapped like a butterfly wing. "That's why I am donating a water purifier to every classroom, and a set of toilets."

(Which you'll notice, Mrs. Naidu, we didn't ask for at all.)

"This afternoon, the electric purifiers will be installed so that the children have drinking water,"

Mrs. Reddy said, shaking her head and sucking her teeth. "The poor things have gone without it too long. As for the toilets, I am currently working with the BEO to install them."

Then Mrs. Reddy picked up a water purifier, put on her best Fevicol-pasted-smile, and posed. The cameras flashed.

"This is what it takes, is it?" Hema Aunty snapped. "A press conference?"

"It's not the media, Hema," Amma said. "It's something far more powerful."

"Rich people?" Hema Aunty asked.

Amma shook her head, and said, "Shame."

"Psssh," Hema Aunty said. "Look at that woman. She has no shame."

"I don't know," Deepti said, "Sujatha Aunty might be right."

We watched as Mrs. Reddy put on a show, posing, holding up the water purifiers that needed electricity that only came once a day, and standing next to the toilets that we had no money to install.

"So she gets to donate toilets, and no one wants to support my tuition program idea?" Amir asked. "Yuck."

"Super yuck," I agreed.

"Who cares?" Deepti said. "Now we have drinking water, and who knows. Maybe we'll even use the toilets. Let her have her photos."

Which I thought was kind of wise, until Deepti yelled at the reporters, "Oy! That's enough."

Finally Vimala Madam made Annie Miss speak, and although her words were wobbly at first, before long, they steadied into her just-and-beautiful-world voice.

"I want to thank everyone for coming together to support our school," she said. "But most of all, I want to honour our students. They are the ones who came up with these ideas. They took it upon themselves to learn about the law, and to lead all of these efforts. I also want to honour the mothers of our community, who are some of the smartest, bravest, toughest women I have ever met. I am so happy and humbled to have gotten to know all of them better, and to have been a small part of this. And I am so, so proud."

Then her voice broke, and she wiped her eyes.

Normally Annie Miss's routine doesn't affect me. But today, my eyes got watery.

(I think I saw Deepti rub her eyes too, Mrs. Naidu. But I wouldn't say that on the record.)

"Child Rights Club members, can you please come up here?" Miss said.

I started to go to the front, when Deepti grabbed Amir's wrist.

"Come on," she said.

"But I'm not in the club," Amir said.

"You're in *our* club," Deepti said.

So I took Amir's right hand, and Deepti took Amir's left hand, and the three of us stood together in front of the flashing cameras. Rohini Reporter stopped clicking and leaned in for a second and said to Deepti, "You were right."

"I was?" Deepti said.

"This *is* a great story," she said.

I looked around the room at all the aunties and Deepti's Appa and Vimala Madam and Amir and Deepti and Annie Miss and Amma and even Mrs. Reddy and the HMs. I looked out the door at the dirt where we were about to dig a playground and the rickshaws full of water purifiers and toilets. I looked at Abhi, who was jumping up and down and clapping, even though he wasn't sure what was going on.

I thought about how in a few years, he might go to a school full of trophies and artwork, where the teachers never hit anyone.

Most of all, I thought about how I was standing in the front of all these reporters holding hands with ~~my best~~ my two best friends.

Do you know what that feels like, Mrs. Naidu?

It feels like forgetting the earth.

It feels like moving the skies.

All the best,
Sarojini

About Mrs. Sarojini Naidu

The book that Sarojini reads about Mrs. Naidu does not actually exist. Luckily, you can learn more about Sarojini Naidu's work as a poet, traveller, freedom fighter, and feminist the same way I did: by reading her own words.

Mrs. Naidu is most famous for her poetry. She has published many books of poems, including *The Golden Threshold*, *The Bird of Time*, and *The Broken Wing*. After Mrs. Naidu's death, her daughter, Padmaja, collected some of her mother's as yet unpublished poems in *The Feather of the Dawn*.

Although Mrs. Naidu considered herself to be a poet first and foremost, she was also a gifted speaker. You can read her speeches in *Sarojini Naidu: Selected Poetry and Prose*, edited by Makarand R. Paranjape, and *Ideas of a Nation (Words of Freedom)* published by Penguin Group.

Finally, just like Sarojini, Mrs. Naidu loved writing letters. You can read some of these in *The Mahatma and the Poetess (Being a Selection of Letters Exchanged Between Gandhiji and Sarojini Naidu)*, compiled by E.S. Reddy and edited by Mrinalini Sarabhai, and

Sarojini Naidu: Selected Letters, 1890s to 1940s, edited
by Makarand R. Paranjape.

Organizations Working for Child Rights

Although this book is a work of fiction, the issues that it deals with are real. In India, a number of groups are working towards helping every child realize his or her rights. Below is a list of organizations where you can get involved and learn more. As Sarojini, Deepti, Amir, and Mrs. Naidu would surely tell you, you're never too young to make a difference.

Childline, India
Tel: 91-22-24952610, 24952611, 24821098, 2490 1098, 24911098
www.childlineindia.org.in
(Visit the website for contact information for local branches.)

Child Rights and You (CRY)
632, Lane No.3, Westend Marg,
Near Saket Metro Station, Saiyad-ul-Ajaib
New Delhi - 110 030.
Tel: 91-11-29533451/52/53
www.cry.org

(Visit the website for contact information for branches in Bangalore, Chennai, Hyderabad, Kolkata, Mumbai/ Pune, and Delhi.)

National Commission for the Protection of Child Rights, Government of India
5th Floor, Chanderlok Building,
36 Janpath, New Delhi-110001
Phone: 91-11-23478200
www.ncpcr.gov.in
(Visit the website for contact information for state chapters of the commission.)

People's Watch
6A, Vallabhai Road, Chokkikulam,
Madurai – 625002,
Phone: 91-452–2539520,
www.peopleswatch.org
(Visit the website for contact information throughout Tamilnadu.)

Right to Education Forum
(On the premises of the Council for Social Development)
53, Sangha Rachna,
Lodi Estate, New Delhi
Phone: 91-11-24615383,   24611700,   24616061,
24693065, 24692655
www.rteforumindia.org/

South Indian Cell for Human Rights Education
35,1st Floor, Anjanappa Complex,
Hennur Main Road, Lingarajapuram,
St. Thomas Town Post,
Bangalore - 560084, Karnataka, India
Phone: 91-80-25473922 / 25804072-73
www.sichrem.org

The Concerned For Working Children
303/2, L B Shastri Nagar Vimanapura Post
Bangalore 560 017
Phone: 91-80-25234611
www.concernedforworkingchildren.org

Acknowledgements

Books may have one author, but they are never created by just one person. So many people helped me bring Sarojini and the gang to life, and it's my honour to thank them here.

Thanks to the Fulbright-Nehru Fellowship office that funded the fieldwork that informed this book. Especially big thanks to Maya Sivakumar, S.K. Bharati, and Vinita Tripathi, the best fellowship administration staff in the world.

Thanks to the ICDS staff, union folks, and anganwadi-going families who let me into their lives. Especially big thanks to Geetha, Sujatha, Sumitra, Varalakshmi, and Yashoda for their patience and friendship, and to their students for putting up with the weird Aunty who sat in the corner for almost two years, watching and asking questions.

Thanks to Chitra Aiyar, Karishma Gulrajani, and Esa Syed for feedback on early drafts. Thanks to Greeshma Patel for co-organizing the photography project that gave me new insight into Bangalore's schools and slums. Special thanks to Dinyar Patel, historical consultant extraordinaire, and Monisha

Bajaj, RTE expert and fairy god-Amma. Extra special thanks to Rohini Mohan for tireless reading and re-reading, afternoons spent working and "working," and doses of encouragement and sanity when I needed them most.

Thanks to Meera Nair for her publishing advice, Minal Hajratwala for her unwavering fairy godmothering, and V.V. Ganeshananthan for her years and years and years of dedicated best friendship (if I could've read this whole book to you over the phone, I would've.) Thanks to Niranjan Aradhya and the team at MAKASA for being my first foray into child-led RTE advocacy. Thanks to Sujatha Akka for the warm meals, Tamil tuitions, and for being the inspiration for Sarojini's Amma.

Thanks to Anita Roy, the editor of every girl's dreams, for her patience, kindness, and generosity, and for the opportunity to publish with Zubaan, a press I have loved for over a decade.

As always, the biggest thanks go to my family. Thanks to Prema Narasimhan (aka mother-in-law) for showing me India and giving me space to write and dream in Coimbatore. Thanks to Bamini Subramanian (aka Mom) for being the inspiration behind every strong woman character I have ever written and will ever write, for putting up with all my writerly and non-writerly drama, and for always believing in me. Thanks to Ram Subramanian (aka thambi) for reading an initial draft, growing up into the feminist little brother I always knew he would become, and being the only person in the world who always gets my jokes. Last, but certainly not least, thanks to Santhosh Ramdoss (aka husband) for moving across the world for me, encouraging me to write this book from the moment it was just a passing thought on the Shatabdi, and standing by my side with encouragement and good humor through this and every other creative endeavor. You are the ones who make me forget the earth, and inspire me to move the skies.